"Dammit, Roxy, what's the matter with you?"

Marcus exploded, "You've blown hot, then cold on me, and I demand to know why!"

"Then I'll tell you!" she shouted back. "I think it's time our relationship ended. I...I don't want to become involved."

"So! It's that old story again about not wanting to be a burden because of your blindness," he mocked. "Well, you won't get away with it!"

What did he mean? "Marcus?" she questioned hoarsely as she felt herself lowered onto the leather sofa. "Marcus, don't...I beg of you!"

"So you don't *want* to become involved," his voice taunted as he bent his head and his lips found hers. "Then tell me how you're planning to accomplish such a feat when you're so deeply involved already."

YVONNE WHITTAL
is also the author of these
Harlequin Romances

and this
Harlequin Presents

Many of these titles are available at your local bookseller.

For a free catalogue listing all available Harlequin Romances
and Harlequin Presents, send your name and address to:

HARLEQUIN READER SERVICE,
1440 South Priest Drive, Tempe, AZ 85281
Canadian address: Stratford, Ontario N5A 6W2

The Light Within

by

YVONNE WHITTAL

Harlequin Books

TORONTO • LONDON • LOS ANGELES • AMSTERDAM
SYDNEY • HAMBURG • PARIS • STOCKHOLM • ATHENS • TOKYO

Original hardcover edition published in 1981
by Mills & Boon Limited

ISBN 0-373-02441-X

Harlequin edition published November 1981

CHAPTER ONE

A car drew up in front of a large grey and white building situated in the centre of Johannesburg, and a girl stepped out on to the pavement, to be followed by a harnessed dog that went swiftly to her side. The girl turned to wave at the man in the car and she waited until he had driven away before walking towards the entrance of the building. Her hair was a rich auburn, waving softly on to slim shoulders, and the slanting rays of the late afternoon sun seemed to finger it with gold. Dark glasses hid her eyes, but her nose was small and straight, her chin rounded and firm, and her mouth was soft and full with the corners lifted as if a permanent smile lurked there.

Roxana Cunningham was beautiful, but she had no way of knowing this. She was equally unaware that her slender figure moved with a natural grace that drew several admiring glances from passers-by. She was also unusually disturbed at that moment, and deep in thought, but the golden labrador at her side led her safely through the glass doors and directly towards the enquiries desk.

'I'll take care of Sheba for you, Miss Cunningham,' the girl at the desk announced, and Roxy smiled and bent down to pat the animal before she released the handle of the harness to walk without hesitation towards the lift.

Her fingers sought the button against the wall, and the mechanised steel doors opened at once. Roxy stepped into the cool, air-conditioned steel cage, and her fingers lightly explored the buttons with practised swiftness to select the correct one. She pressed it, and the doors slid shut. She waited for that familiar 'click', and then she was being swept up to the fourth floor.

She knew this building as well as she knew her own home. She had come here too often over the years to call on her father not to feel totally confident of finding her way about without Sheba's valued assistance. But today was different.

Roxy felt disturbed and unhappy after her session with Noreen Butler that afternoon, and when she finally stepped out of the lift, her level of concentration was at its lowest. She turned left into the carpeted corridor, walking swiftly in her agitation, and collided so heavily with a solid male frame that she almost succeeded in knocking the breath from her body.

'I'm most dreadfully sorry,' she apologised unsteadily on shaky legs when she had recovered from the shock of the collision to find strong hands supporting her. She was conscious of several things in that split second of coming to her senses; the roughness of tweed beneath her fingers, the faint odour of his masculine cologne, and something else she could not define—an awareness, perhaps, that quivered along her nerves like a slow current of electricity.

'I don't usually make a habit of walking into people,' she tried again, sensing his annoyance, and then those strong hands were setting her aside roughly.

'Perhaps if you removed those infernal dark glasses you'd be able to see where you are going,' a deep, well-modulated voice accused.

'That wouldn't make the slightest difference,' she replied, amusement lifting the corners of her mouth. 'I'm blind, you see.'

'In that case you shouldn't be wandering about without an assistant,' he retorted, not sounding in the least put out by her revelation and, against her will, Roxy was intrigued.

'My assistant is waiting downstairs in the lobby,' she informed him. 'She's of the four-legged variety, and very reliable, but she knows her place.'

'Whom did you wish to see?'

He used the word 'see' without hesitation, or embarrassment, and Roxy was becoming more than just ordinarily interested in this stranger she had almost floored a few minutes ago.

'I'm going to see Theodore Cunningham. His office is four doors down from here, I think.'

'That's correct.' His voice sounded clipped; impatient almost. 'Do you think you'll find your way there without trampling some other poor unsuspecting person?'

'I shall do my best.'

She felt him withdraw and, totally flustered by her encounter with this man, waited until she heard the lift doors close behind him before she attempted to make her way a little more carefully down the corridor towards the offices of Cunningham & Fraser, Attorneys at Law.

'Hello, my dear,' her father greeted her when she entered his office a few minutes later. 'How did you get here?'

'Basil gave me a lift so that I could go home with you.' She paused, tried to shake off her own problems, and asked: 'Have you had a busy day?'

'Reasonably so,' Theodore admitted, and she heard his chair creak as it always did when he leaned back in it. 'You look a bit harassed. What's up?'

'Oh——' she sighed, and shrugged, adding vaguely,

'I had a particularly depressing afternoon, and I'm afraid I almost ploughed through someone in the corridor a few minutes ago.'

'You went to see one of Basil Vaughn's patients this afternoon?'

She nodded, and then she could no longer keep it to herself. 'A young mother of two small children who was blinded by acid. She'll receive financial compensation, naturally, from the firm where she'd been employed, but——'

'Don't, Roxy,' her father interrupted, and his chair creaked again as he got up and came to her side to place an arm about her shoulders. 'Don't tear yourself apart like this.'

Roxy buried her face against the expensive material of his jacket, and inhaled the familiar, comforting scent of him. 'I just wish there was something I could do for her.'

'You *are* doing something,' Theodore insisted with some urgency. 'You're helping this poor woman to adjust to this new situation, and that's very important.'

'Acceptance isn't something someone else can give you. It's something you have to find for yourself.'

'*You* know that, and *I* know it, but with the necessary courage, determination and confidence it can be achieved. You can help her, Roxy, but only if your determination and confidence remain intact. Lose faith in yourself, and others will lose faith in what you're trying to do.'

It all made wonderful sense, but there were times, such as this, when her helpless inadequacy filled her with futile bitterness.

'Don't lose heart, Roxy,' her father continued. 'Just go on trying, and good sense will win through in the end.'

She wrapped her arms about his waist and hugged him. 'What would I do without you, Daddy?'

'You'd find someone else to lecture you.'

He said it so matter-of-factly that she laughed, and minutes later she left the office with him and went down in the lift to collect Sheba at the desk in the lobby.

When Theodore went out after dinner that evening, Roxy took Sheba for her usual run in the garden, but the autumn night was chilly, and they entered the house through the french windows fifteen minutes later.

The house was silent except for the muted sounds of the servants moving about in the kitchen, and Roxy sat down in her favourite chair in the living-room, her hand idly stroking the labrador's smooth head until the animal flopped down at her feet and remained there, sleepy, yet alert to anything or anyone who might wish to harm her mistress.

Roxy often spent her evenings listening to records, but this evening her thoughts were in too much of a turmoil to appreciate good music. She thought of Noreen Butler lying there in the clinic, and the woman's despondency became a part of her. She had spent almost three hours with her that afternoon, talking, encouraging, and listening as the woman poured out her bitterness and her fears. Nothing Roxy had said had seemed to make the slightest impression, and she had been almost relieved when Basil had come into the ward and announced that it was time to leave.

The snap of a light switch interrupted her thoughts, and an irate voice demanded, 'Miss Roxy, why are you sitting here all alone in the darkness?'

Roxy shrugged listlessly. 'Light or darkness, it's all the same.'

'Tch!' The woman who had been Roxy's personal maid and chauffeur for the past ten years approached the chair in her slippered feet. 'Who's been upsetting you again?'

'I was thinking,' Roxy replied absently. 'If I should ever marry someone . . .'

'Of course you'll get married, Miss Roxy.'

'If I should ever marry and have children, I'll never know what they look like,' Roxy continued, ignoring the interruption. 'How terrible it must be for someone who was able to *see* her children, and then to find that she'll never be able to see them again.'

'What are you talking about, Miss Roxy?'

'Oh, it doesn't matter, Maggie,' Roxy sighed, fingering the dial of her wrist watch and finding to her surprise that it was after ten. 'It's time I went to bed.' She got to her feet and so did the labrador. A wet nose was pushed into her palm, and she fondled the animal's head lovingly for a moment before she straightened. 'Will you see to Sheba for me, Maggie?'

'Yes, Miss Roxy. Come along, Sheba, it's time you went to bed too.'

Roxy gave Sheba a gentle pat on the hindquarters, and she followed Maggie obediently, her large paws padding softly over the carpeted floor.

Light and darkness. Going from the one into the other had been swift and painful, and she had woken up in hospital ten years ago to learn that she would never see the light again. As a twelve-year-old she had been unobservant, taking the beauty of her surroundings very much for granted. Now, at the age of twenty-two, she wondered if her memory of certain things was to be trusted. How could she be sure in this world of darkness what it was like to lie on your back in the tall grass, staring up at the blue sky, and watching the clouds change shape from second to second? Was everything truly as she remembered it?

She paid Noreen Butler a visit every afternoon during the rest of that week, and the week after, and

Dr Basil Vaughn was more than pleased with the results she was obtaining.

When she walked into Noreen's ward one Friday afternoon, she found her seated beside the open window and joined her there in the chair Basil had placed at her disposal before departing. They talked for a long time about Noreen's children, about her husband, and the news that he had found a job closer to home, then, after a thoughtful silence, Noreen said: 'I suppose you know Dr Vaughn thinks I'm well enough to be transferred to the Lockhart Clinic tomorrow.'

'No, I didn't know,' Roxy replied, hiding her pleasure at this unexpected news. 'How do you feel about it?'

'Nervous.'

'At the Lockhart Clinic they'll help you to regain a great deal of your self-confidence and independence. You'll learn to read Braille, and how to exploit your other senses.'

'I know.' Noreen sounded excited. 'Dr Vaughn says it's almost like taking a refresher course at school.'

'In many ways it is,' Roxy laughed, remembering her own childhood experiences in a place of that nature.

There was a long silence, disturbed only by the hum of activity in the adjoining wards, then Noreen said hesitantly, 'Miss Cunningham—Roxy—I don't suppose we'll meet again, but I—I want you to know that I appreciate what you've done for me. I realise I'm now going to be placed in the hands of people who've specialised in this sort of thing, but none of them could have helped me as much as you've done during these past weeks. I think I can face the future now, and I have you to thank for that.'

'Noreen . . .' Roxy reached across the distance separating them and found the woman's hands with her own, 'I'm happy that I could have helped you in some way. It's good to feel that I can still be useful.'

'Useful *and* needed,' Noreen replied, her hands tightening about Roxy's. 'Yes, that's important. To feel you're still of some use to those around you, and to be needed as I needed you, and as my family still need me.'

When Basil called for Roxy a few minutes later, he asked: 'Can you spare a few minutes before I drive you home?'

'Yes, of course,' she said at once, and he led her swiftly down one passage and yet another while he explained:

'There's an eight-year-old boy in the children's wing. He refuses to talk, and he refuses to eat, and we're having a hell of a time trying to convince him it's not the end of the world.'

'How did it happen?'

'He was playing with his father's rifle when it went off, and if he's lucky he'll have partial vision in the one eye, but I can't even guarantee that at this moment.'

'How on earth did he get hold of such a weapon?'

'Gross negligence on the father's side, if you ask me—and then they expect me to perform miracles,' Basil replied, his voice harsh with anger. 'I've put the young fellow into a private ward for the time being until he's able to cope with having other children about,' he added as he ushered Roxy through a door and towards the high hospital bed.

The nurse in attendance muttered something about leaving them alone, and went out with a swish of her starched skirt, then Basil said brightly, 'Hello, Chris. I've brought a visitor to meet you.'

'Hello, Chris,' Roxy began, but her tentative greeting was met with silence, and if her sensitive ears had not picked up the sound of the child's shallow breathing, she would have imagined herself addressing the wall. 'My name is Roxy,' she tried again, and again there was silence. 'I know, you don't feel like talking much, but if you don't say something, I shan't recognise you again. You see, I'm blind, but I've learnt to know people by the sound of their voices.'

The silence intensified for a moment, and then a clear, childish voice said sharply, 'I wish I was dead!'

'You shouldn't wish that, Chris,' Roxy said hastily, but she could not help recalling her own bitterness ten years ago. 'Chris?'

There was silence once again, and this time Basil intervened with a touch of impatience in his voice. 'Come on, Roxy. Young Master Chris has tuned out on us.'

Basil drove her to her father's Houghton home in an angry silence, and it was well after seven when he pulled up in front of the house.

'Damn!' he exclaimed, thumping the steering wheel with his fist and making her jump. 'Young Chris isn't responding to treatment, and I feel as though my hands are tied.'

'He needs an interest; something to make him realise there's still so much to live for.'

'I agree with you. But what is there we could interest him in?'

'I wonder . . .' she began as a thought occurred to her, then she discarded the idea, but decided eventually to risk making the suggestion. 'Do you think you could persuade the authorities to bend their rules a little so that Sheba could go in with me next time I visit Chris?'

Sheba, hearing her name mentioned, sat up in the back of the car and nuzzled Roxy's neck.

If Basil was startled by her suggestion then he gave no indication of it, and merely asked a little dubiously,

'Do you think he might respond more to a dog?'

'I've yet to meet a child who doesn't respond to an animal of some sort,' she laughed, ducking away from Sheba's cold nose in her neck.

'It's worth a try, I suppose,' Basil admitted with growing enthusiasm.

'*I* think it's worth it.'

He took a moment to make up his mind, then he said firmly, 'I'll have a chat to the Superintendent and the Matron first thing tomorrow, then I'll give you a ring.'

'I shall be waiting anxiously to hear from you,' Roxy told him as she got out of the car and opened the back door for Sheba to alight. 'Thanks for the lift, Basil.'

He drove away at speed, and before Roxy could instruct Sheba to take her inside, Maggie came quickly down the steps to meet her.

'You're late, Miss Roxy,' she said a little breathlessly. 'Did you forget your father was having guests over for dinner this evening?'

'Oh, dear,' Roxy sighed guiltily. 'It slipped my mind completely, and I suppose Daddy nearly had a fit.'

'He was worried, Miss Roxy.'

'Yes, I suppose so,' she agreed with remorse. 'Let's go in the back way, then you can help me change quickly into something more suitable.'

Upstairs in her bedroom Roxy took a quick shower and changed into the long-sleeved evening dress Maggie had selected for her. Maggie fastened the single string of pearls about Roxy's neck and brushed the life back into her hair, then she stood aside and watched critically while Roxy applied her own make-up; something which had taken long hours of practice before she had accomplished it to her own, and Maggie's, satisfaction.

'How do I look?' Roxy asked a little apprehensively.

'Beautiful, Miss Roxy. The green of your dress matches your eyes, but no one will notice when you're always hiding them behind those dark glasses.'

Roxy smiled tolerantly and turned towards the door, her movements confident and sure. 'I'd better get myself downstairs, or Daddy might *really* have a fit!'

She walked slowly down the passage, turned left at the head of the stairs and, with her hand sliding lightly along the banister, she descended into the hall. Judging by the crescendo of voices, her father had invited quite a crowd to dinner that evening. She disliked crowds intensely; it made her nervous, but, for her father's sake, she always put in an appearance, and usually excused herself long before the first guests departed.

Quick, agitated footsteps crossed the hall towards her. 'For heaven's sake, Roxy, where have you been?'

'I'm sorry, Daddy. There was this little boy, and——' She bit her lips and gestured vaguely with her hands. 'I'll explain later.'

'You're too late for dinner, but we're having coffee in the living-room,' Theodore explained, taking her arm and drawing her towards the source of the noise.

Several familiar voices said 'hello' and chatted while Theodore poured a cup of coffee and placed it in Roxy's hands, then she sensed someone else's presence close to her, and there was a certain urgency in her father's hand as he drew her a little aside.

'Roxy, I'd like you to meet a client of mine, Marcus Fleming. He's the director of Phoenix Engineering. Marcus, my daughter Roxana.'

A strong hand clasped Roxy's. 'How do you do, Miss Cunningham.'

That voice! Well modulated, and deep with a resonant timbre, it struck a familiar and disturbing chord in her memory.

'But we've met before,' she said a little breathlessly. 'And quite violently, if I remember correctly.'

'In the corridor leading to Theodore's office—yes,' Marcus Fleming acknowledged with a hint of a smile in his voice.

'Good heavens, Roxy, was it Marcus you ploughed into the other day?' her father wanted to know.

'I'm afraid so,' she admitted, her cheeks growing warm.

'Well, I'll leave the two of you together then to make your peace,' her father laughed, and suddenly she found herself alone with Marcus Fleming and wishing for some peculiar reason that she could run and hide somewhere.

'You surprise me, Miss Cunningham,' his amused voice cut across her frantic thoughts of escape.

'Why?' she asked, trying to control the quiver of alarm that raced through her. 'Does it surprise you that I should have recognised your voice?'

'Our meeting was very brief, and it occurred more than two weeks ago.'

'You were very rude, I remember.'

'Was I?'

Again there was that suggestion of a smile in his voice, and the corners of her mouth lifted in response. 'Not really. You were most polite, considering I did everything but kick you in the shins.'

'How magnanimous of you to say so!' he drawled.

She tilted her head thoughtfully in the direction of his voice. 'I think you're mocking me, Mr Fleming, and that's unkind of you.'

'I don't have a reputation for kindness,' he said abruptly. 'The best I could manage is pity.'

Roxy felt herself shrink inwardly. 'I don't object to kindness, but I draw the line at pity.'

'You consider yourself quite self-sufficient, then?'

'When you say it like that you make me sound awfully smug,' she laughed nervously, 'but I try not to be a nuisance to my family and friends.'

'Does it hurt your pride to have to rely on others?'

'Yes ... and no.' She paused briefly to wonder whether this man was deliberately baiting her, or genuinely interested, then she said: 'I prefer to manage on my own, but there are times when I'm forced to rely on others. That's the most difficult part of being blind, I think. I'm fiercely independent by nature, and prefer to do things for myself.' She had not intended to say so much, but somehow it had all come out. 'I don't know why I'm telling you all this. I must be boring you to tears, and I assure you that I don't normally discuss myself this freely with strangers.'

'Are you suggesting we discuss the weather?'

An uncertain smile hovered on her lips. 'That wouldn't be in your line at all.'

'What makes you so certain of that?'

'You're not a man for platitudes.' She hesitated, wondering whether she had gone too far, but when he remained silent as if waiting for her to continue, she added: 'There's a thread of impatience in your voice that suggests you're a man for action, and not for the social niceties which most people seem to expect and thrive on.' She hesitated again, then asked curiously, 'Am I right?'

'Quite remarkably so, yes,' he laughed briefly. 'Functions such as this one call for politeness, and being polite can often be a strain.'

'Do you feel you have to be polite to me because

you're a guest in my father's home?' she asked with a mixture of humour and seriousness.

'Are you fishing for compliments?'

'No . . . the truth.'

The din of voices grew louder during the brief ensuing silence, and then he said quite bluntly, 'I wasn't being polite. I was being downright curious.'

Roxy could not explain why she should feel relieved, but she did, and she could not resist the temptation to ask, 'What happens now that you've satisfied your curiosity?'

'I get you a fresh cup of coffee. You've let this one get cold,' he said as he took the cup from her hands and placed it on the trolley beside them, but she hastily prevented him from pouring out a fresh cup of Maggie's rich aromatic brew.

'I didn't really want anything to drink in the first place.'

Marcus Fleming was standing close to her—too close, she decided as her senses became alert to his particular brand of masculine cologne. His hand touched her arm, and again she felt that surge of awareness she had experienced that day in the corridor outside her father's office.

'Do you think your father would think it rude if we slipped outside for a while?' he asked close to her ear.

She experienced a brief moment of uncertainty, then she said: 'He's so busy debating whether some poor fellow is guilty or not that I doubt if we would be missed.'

'Then shall we seek the peace and quiet of the garden?'

She nodded silently and allowed him to guide her from the room, and out on to the terrace. The tightening of his hand on her arm was a clear indication to her that they had reached the steps leading down into the scented garden. He had done so naturally, and silently, and for the first time she relaxed fractionally in his company.

They followed the path down to the fishpond, but before they reached it Roxy's ears detected the sound of Sheba's heavy panting, and she called the dog to her side.

'Mr Fleming, meet my most valued assistant,' she said lightly. 'Sheba, say "hello" to Mr Fleming.'

'Well, I'll be——!' He broke off sharply, and a moment later asked with amazement, 'Does she usually give her paw to people?'

'Only if she finds them acceptable,' Roxy smiled. 'Sheba takes the place of my eyes, and she can normally sense instinctively when someone is a threat to me in any way.'

'I take it, then, that she likes me?'

'She's bestowed upon you the honour of taking her paw, and few people receive that honour.'

'How long have you had her?' he asked.

'Four years.'

'She's a beauty.'

'So I'm told,' Roxy replied without rancour or bitterness. 'There's a bench just along here. Shall we sit down?'

'Have you always been blind?' he asked directly once they were seated.

'No.' Her fingers absently caressed Sheba's big head resting in her lap. 'I lost my sight ten years ago when I was twelve.'

'Why do you wear those dark glasses?'

She stiffened with a measure of resentment. 'Why do you ask so many questions?'

'Would you prefer it if I deliberately avoided the subject of your blindness?'

There was an indefinable thread of steel in that beautiful voice, and she considered his question carefully before saying with complete sincerity, 'You're the first man I've known, other than my father and Dr Vaughn, who doesn't feel uncomfortable in my company.'

'I don't see why I should feel uncomfortable. I feel quite secure in the knowledge that you can't see the third eye in the middle of my forehead, my broken nose, and my buck teeth.'

'Don't be silly!' she laughed.

'You see?' he mocked her. 'You've already attached a face to my voice, and I could be as ugly as sin and you wouldn't know it.'

She had never met a man like Marcus Fleming before who could put her so at ease, and she said thoughtfully, 'You intrigue me.'

'You've stolen my line,' he accused shortly.

'Your line?'

'The man usually tells the woman that he finds her intriguing when he's actually trying to tell her that she's beautiful.'

Roxy felt a strange stirring in her breast. Was she beautiful? Her father and Maggie were always telling her so, but was she truly beautiful, or were they merely trying to appease her?

'You're mocking me again, I think,' she said uncertainly.

'And you haven't answered my question,' he returned swiftly, his arm brushing against hers and sending those little sparks of awareness quivering through her. 'Why do you hide behind those dark glasses?'

'People usually find it disconcerting when I look beyond them, or stare fixedly at their noses,' she told him selfconsciously.

'Unless they have warts on their noses, I can't see why it should bother them, or you, for that matter.'

Her soft laughter rang out clearly in the silent, moonlit garden. 'I never thought of it like that before.'

'What do you do with yourself all day?' he continued to question her, and she decided suddenly that she did not mind if he did.

'In the mornings I work at home, transcribing books into Braille, and in the afternoons I visit patients at the eye clinic who've lost their sight.'

'So you're a part-time social worker.'

'I wouldn't describe myself as such,' she corrected with a touch of humility. 'I help them with the process of adjusting to their blindness, or I try to.'

'Do you have much success?'

'Basil seems to think so.'

'Basil?'

'Dr Vaughn,' she explained, wondering whether she had imagined that Marcus Fleming had suddenly grown tense beside her. 'He's an eye specialist, and he happens to be my doctor as well as my employer and friend.'

'Do you go to the clinic every day of the week?' he asked, his voice giving nothing away.

'I go whenever I'm needed, or whenever I feel it necessary to spend more time with a patient.'

'What do you do for recreation?'

He sounded like an over-curious journalist, she thought with a touch of wry humour, but she answered him nevertheless. 'I play chess, and I listen to records.'

'What about coming out to Hartebeespoort Dam with me on Sunday? We could take a boat out on the dam, and have a picnic lunch somewhere shady.'

The invitation was so unexpected and so sudden that she was momentarily at a loss for words.

'Don't you like the idea?' he asked abruptly, and she pulled herself together with an effort.

'I've never been on a boat before,' she explained hesitantly. 'Well . . . not since I was a child, and I . . .'

'You'll be quite safe with me,' he assured her, almost as if he had guessed her fears. 'Will you come?'

Roxy had a peculiar feeling that she had reached some sort of crossroads in her life. If she refused his invitation there was a strong possibility that they might never meet again, and if she accepted, it could lead to something she had tried to avoid up till now. There was something about Marcus Fleming that made him stand out above all the other men she had known. It was something indefinable, but she could feel herself being drawn as if by a magnet, and although her common sense urged her to refuse, there was another part of her that urged her to do the opposite.

'I think I would like to accept your invitation,' she said quickly before she could change her mind.

'That's settled then,' he said at once. 'I'll pick you up at ten this Sunday morning.'

They remained outside in the garden for a little while longer, but when the night air became too chilly he took her inside, and Sheba, feeling neglected, went round to her kennel at the back of the house.

Marcus Fleming did not stay long after that, and when he sought her out to say goodnight, she smiled up at him and said: 'I shall look forward to Sunday, Mr Fleming.'

'The name's Marcus,' he said lightly, his fingers tightening briefly about hers, and her cheeks grew warm as he added: 'Goodnight, Roxy.'

CHAPTER TWO

ROXY was having breakfast the following morning when Basil Vaughn telephoned to say that he had received permission for her to bring Sheba into the clinic.

'Did you have difficulty persuading them?' she asked curiously.

'Don't ask questions,' he laughed briefly. 'Just bring that animal here this afternoon, and pray that your idea works.'

Roxy's hand tightened on the receiver. 'You sound anxious.'

'Young Chris is being fed intravenously at the moment, and I don't like the look of him,' Basil replied in a clipped tone. 'To add to my problems, I've had to refuse his mother permission to see him because she will insist on having hysterics and upsetting the child further.'

'And the father?'

'Blaming himself, naturally, but still as cocky as hell.'

The line seemed to crackle with Basil's frustration and anger, and Roxy frowned. 'I'll do the best I can, Basil.'

'I know you will,' he announced, and moments later Roxy replaced the receiver on its cradle.

She could not eat anything after that, and settled instead for a cup of coffee while she tried to work out some plan of action, but she had never dealt with a child before, and she was totally at a loss.

She spent the rest of the morning preparing herself for her visit to the clinic in the afternoon. Sheba, too, received her fair share of attention, and displayed remarkable indulgence while Roxy and Maggie gave her a thorough shampoo. After lunch that day, Roxy went out on to the back lawn once more to give Sheba's coat a final brush, and it was there that Maggie found her when it was time to leave.

'My goodness, Miss Roxy, is it a special occasion for Sheba?'

'I'm taking her into the clinic this afternoon to meet a little boy,' Roxy explained nervously.

'Well, for goodness' sake, Miss Roxy, if you go on brushing her like that, she won't have any hair left!'

Roxy put down the brush and ran her hands lightly over Sheba's smooth coat. 'Does she look all right?'

'She always looks fine to me, Miss Roxy,' Maggie laughed throatily. 'Shall I put Sheba's harness on while you get yourself ready?'

'If you would, please, Maggie,' Roxy smiled, getting up off her knees. 'See that she doesn't dirty herself while I go inside to wash my hands and dump this overall.'

Less than a half hour later they arrived at the clinic, and Roxy felt more than just a little apprehensive when she climbed out of the car with Sheba.

'I may be long, Maggie,' she warned.

'I'll wait, Miss Roxy,' Maggie assured her. 'I always bring my embroidery with me to keep myself occupied.'

Roxy nodded slightly, and a few seconds later she was confronted on the steps by the nurse on duty at Reception. 'Dr Vaughn said I was to take you to the child as soon as you arrived, Miss Cunningham.'

'Thank you,' Roxy murmured with a nervous smile. 'If you go on ahead then Sheba will follow.'

She felt decidedly shaky when she eventually stood beside Chris's bed. It was so very important that she should succeed that she was almost taut with nerves.

'Chris?' she whispered the child's name, but she heard nothing except his shallow breathing, and her heart began to thud anxiously. 'I'm Roxy. Do you remember me? I came to visit you yesterday, and I've brought along a very special visitor for you today.' Still no response, and, taking the final plunge, she said softly, 'Sheba, give Chris a *big* hello.'

Sheba needed no further encouragement. She knew what a *big* hello meant, and she barked twice, the sound reverberating round the small, silent ward.

The child's breathing altered at once, became almost agitated, and then, to Roxy's relief, he said in a weak, incredulous voice, 'It's a dog!'

'Yes, Sheba's a dog,' Roxy replied, crossing her fingers and praying silently that she was doing the right thing. 'She's a golden labrador, and they say she's beautiful, but I can tell that by the smoothness of her coat.' She hesitated briefly, trying to sense the child's reaction, then she said: 'Would you like to stroke her?'

There was a frightening little silence, then Chris surprised her by asking, 'May I?'

'Of course you may,' Roxy replied at once. 'Up, Sheba!'

Sheba obeyed at once and, standing on her hind legs, placed her front paws on the immaculately white bed. Roxy found Chris's hand and guided it towards Sheba's head.

'Her nose is wet,' he announced at once.

'Feel how soft her ears are,' Roxy laughed, guiding

the child's hand, and Sheba placidly allowed her ears to be fondled by Chris's small fingers.

'Is she your dog?' he asked after a while.

'Yes,' Roxy replied at once, not yet able to believe the success she was having. 'Sheba's a very special dog.'

'Why is she special?'

'She's a guide dog.'

'What's a guide dog?' Chris wanted to know.

'She leads me where I want to go, and she makes sure that I don't bump into things, or fall down steps, and so on. You see,' she added gently, 'Sheba takes the place of my eyes.'

'I saw a movie once of a dog leading a man across the street,' said Chris. 'Can Sheba do that?'

'Oh, yes,' Roxy assured him. 'She watches the traffic lights for me, and when they turn green she takes me safely across the street.'

'Does she have one of those handles on for you to hold on to?'

'Yes, she has.' There was a little silence, and then she heard Chris sigh. 'Are you tired?'

'Yes,' he whispered.

'I'll leave you, then,' Roxy murmured, ordering Sheba to remove her paws from the bed.

'Roxy?'

'Yes, Chris?'

There was an awkward little silence, then he asked, 'Will you come again?'

Roxy's heart lifted. 'I'll come again tomorrow.'

'And Sheba?'

'I had to get special permission to bring her in today, but if you get better quickly Dr Vaughn will let you sit in the garden outside, then I'll bring her to you every day.' She found his small hand and squeezed his fingers lightly. 'Okay?'

'Okay.'

Roxy's step was much lighter when Sheba took her back the way they had come, but when she reached the car Maggie said almost accusingly, 'You're crying, Miss Roxy.'

'Oh,' Roxy exclaimed in a surprised and faintly choked voice, 'I'm being silly, I suppose.'

'Is that little boy very sick?' Maggie wanted to know as she started the car and set it in motion.

'Not sick, Maggie. Just embittered, and very scared, I think.'

'When it happened to you, Miss Roxy, were you scared too?'

'Very scared,' Roxy admitted, biting her lip. 'It was like a living death at first, and then, gradually, it became easier to bear.'

'You mean, Miss Roxy, it's like eating pumpkin when you're a child. You hate it, but when you get older it doesn't taste too bad.'

'Something like that,' Roxy laughed, leaning back in her seat and trying to ease the tension from her muscles.

Roxy was still a little dubious of her success when Basil telephoned her that evening. 'I thought you'd like to know that young Chris ate a hearty dinner this evening,' he said, 'and when I saw him a few minutes ago he wanted to know how soon he could get up so that he could sit in the garden and play with Sheba.'

'Oh, Basil . . .' Roxy was too choked for a moment to speak, and swallowing convulsively, she said eventually, 'I'm so glad.'

'I sometimes wonder what I would do without you,' Basil laughed, his relief evident.

'You'll find someone else,' she told him promptly.

'I'm so relieved, I think I'll add a bonus on to your

cheque at the end of the month.'

'Oh, no! Please don't do that!'

'I'll save it for Christmas, then,' he laughed away her protest. 'Goodnight, Roxy.'

Roxy replaced the receiver and returned to her chair in the living-room. She felt more than ordinarily pleased with the outcome of her visit to Chris that afternoon, and when Sheba padded up to her chair, Roxy gave her a joyous hug.

'We did it, Sheba! We did it!' she cried softly, and Sheba whined in her throat as if she knew exactly what Roxy was talking about.

'You're not concentrating, Roxy,' her father accused later that evening when they were playing chess on the board he had had specially designed for her. 'I've just taken your knight with my bishop and placed your king in check.'

Roxy smiled inwardly. 'I was hoping you'd do that. Now I can move my rook into position to protect my king, and it's checkmate, I think.'

'Well, of all the——!' Theodore spluttered, then he laughed sourly. 'Dammit, Roxy, you could at least let me win sometimes.'

Roxy pushed aside the chess table and leaned back in her chair, and her eyes, almost a clear emerald green, stared vacantly up at the ceiling. It had been an exciting day, one way and another, and she felt pleasantly tired. She could hear her father moving about and could hear the clink of glasses. They ended most evenings in this manner; with a glass of wine and a chat before going to bed. It was a pleasant ritual, and one she seldom enjoyed missing.

'Your wine,' said Theodore, and when she felt the glass touch her hand, her fingers curled about the stem.

'Thank you, Daddy.' She raised her glass, sniffed

lightly at the contents, and then took a sip. 'Hm . . .' she smiled with satisfaction. 'Riesling, semi-sweet.'

'You're getting much too clever,' her father teased goodnaturedly as he resumed his seat opposite her.

'Tell me about Marcus Fleming,' she said eventually. 'How long have you known him?'

If Theodore was surprised at this request, he gave no sign of it as he said: 'I've known Marcus for about two months, but I knew his uncle, William Fleming, much better. I've been handling Phoenix Engineering's legal problems for eight years now. William died a little over two months ago, and that was when Marcus took over the directorship. William always spoke very highly of Marcus.'

'Is that all?' Roxy asked a little disappointedly when her father lapsed into silence.

'What else do you want to know?' Theodore laughed.

'Anything and everything that there is to know about him,' she replied without embarrassment.

'Well, let me see,' he began thoughtfully. 'Marcus is thirty-five, and there's hardly a country in the world he hasn't visited. He speaks seven different languages fluently, and he did a bit of motor racing once, but gave it up when a friend of his died on the track. He plays squash, enjoys yachting and mountaineering, and I believe he's a deadly opponent when it comes to karate. I know that women appear to favour him, because my secretary is in a constant swoon when he's about, and I believe he never lacks female company.' Roxy sat there with the odd feeling that someone had winded her, then her father asked abruptly, 'Why are you so interested?'

She swallowed down the last of her wine, then twirled the stem of her glass between nervous fingers. 'He's invited me to go out to Hartebeespoort Dam with him tomorrow for the day.'

'I see.' The clock ticked loudly on the mantelshelf. 'Are you going?'

'I said I would, but now you've told me about him I'm wondering whether it would be wise.'

'You could always take Sheba along for protection,' Theodore suggested humorously.

Roxy grimaced. 'The trouble is, Sheba likes him.'

'Oh, dear!'

'Don't laugh, Daddy,' she said reprovingly. 'This is serious.'

'Serious?'

'Why should a man like Marcus Fleming bother with someone like myself when there are plenty of girls obviously hankering for his company?'

'For heaven's sake, Roxy,' her father exploded, 'why shouldn't he bother with you? You're an attractive girl, and I can assure you that you have all the right things in the right places.' He was silent for a moment, then he added roughly, 'That was supposed to make you laugh.'

Her jaw went rigid. 'For a man who leads such an active life, a blind companion could only become an irritating burden.'

'Roxy,' her father began with a hint of impatience in his gravelly voice, 'the man has asked you to go out with him . . . nothing more. Let him decide for himself whether you're a burden or not.'

'By that time it might be too late.'

'Too late for what?' he asked suspiciously.

'How should I know?' she replied irritably, placing her empty glass on the small table beside her chair and getting to her feet. She walked across to the window and opened it, welcoming the cool air against her cheeks. 'I've been out with men before,' she explained without turning. 'Our association seldom lasted beyond the first date. They felt uncomfortable, and I knew it, but Marcus Fleming is different.'

Her father got up from his chair and joined her at the window. 'Are you afraid you might fall in love with him?'

A little shock went through Roxy. Falling in love with Marcus Fleming had never entered her head, but becoming too deeply involved with him had. Did that amount to the same thing? she wondered confusedly as she said a little harshly, 'I'd be a fool if I *did* fall in love with him.'

'I'd like to see you married, Roxy,' her father stated calmly, placing an arm about her shoulders. 'I'd like to know that when I'm no longer there, there'll be someone to take care of you.'

'I can take care of myself,' she said stubbornly, and he shook her slightly.

'Yes, you independent hussy, but I'd like to see you married all the same, and it would have to be to someone who could control you.'

'I don't need controlling!' she cried indignantly.

'I'm not going to argue with you, my dear,' her father laughed, kissing her on the cheek. 'Let's go up to bed.'

Roxy paid an early visit to the clinic on the Sunday morning to see Chris, and found him in a surprisingly cheerful mood. He sounded much stronger, and the nursing Sister told Roxy that if he continued to regain his strength in that manner he would soon be allowed out of bed for certain periods of the day.

'You will remember your promise to come and see me every day?' he asked when she was about to leave.

'I'll remember,' Roxy assured him, and, raising his

hand to her lips, she whispered, 'See you tomorrow, Chris.'

Roxy felt much happier about him now, but she had been home only a few minutes when Maggie came up to her room to tell her that Marcus Fleming was waiting downstairs for her, and her thoughts of Chris were shifted temporarily into the background.

Nervously she went down to meet him, but as she stepped into the hall he came towards her and at once took her hand. 'I'm a bit early.'

'I don't mind,' she said quickly, finding it disturbing that he should continue holding her hand in such a familiar manner.

'Are you ready to go?'

She nodded silently, and a few minutes later she was seated in his car. Her hands explored the seat covering. It felt expensive, luxurious, and then the engine purred into life and the car was set in motion.

'You're driving fast,' she said a few minutes later.

'Yes,' he said abruptly. 'Does speed worry you?'

'Not when I can feel that the person in control knows what he's doing, as you obviously do.'

'It's a perfect day for a picnic,' he changed the subject. 'There's hardly a cloud in the sky.'

'I never asked,' she said apologetically now. 'Shouldn't I have brought along something for our lunch?'

'You're *my* guest today,' Marcus insisted calmly, 'and Carlo always packs a perfect lunch.'

'Carlo?'

'Carlo Vicente owns a restaurant in Hillbrow, and he's an old friend of mine,' Marcus explained.

Roxy lapsed into silence, and they talked very little after that during the hour-long drive to the dam, but the silence was not uncomfortable, although she was continually conscious of his disturbing presence beside her.

'We're not far from where the boat is moored,' he told her when he had parked the car and helped her out.

'Is it your boat, or have you hired it?' she asked, allowing him to take her arm and guide her along the path towards the water's edge.

'It belongs to a friend.'

'You have many friends?' she asked a little teasingly.

'Several,' he answered abruptly, his hand tightening on her arm, and holding her back. 'There are three steps,' he warned her in the same tone of voice.

Roxy negotiated the narrow steps without difficulty to find herself walking on what seemed to be a wooden platform with the sound of the water beneath her feet.

'Stay here,' said Marcus, placing her hands on a rough wooden railing in front of her, and her hands tightened their grip nervously.

He moved away from her, and she heard him jump down on to something solid which she suspected had to be the boat when she heard the disturbed water lapping against its side.

'Marcus?' she questioned nervously, her body tensing at the thought of what he would soon expect of her.

'I'll be with you in a minute,' he said tersely, and a few moments later she felt him take her hands and draw her a little away from the railing. He was not standing on the same level as herself, she could judge that by the direction of his voice when he finally placed his hands about her waist and said: 'Put your hands on my shoulders for support. I'm going to lift you down into the boat.'

She swallowed nervously, cold despite the heat of the sun, and slid her hands up two muscular arms until they came to rest on his shoulders, then the muscles rippled beneath her fingers as she felt herself being lifted through the air as if she had weighed no more than a child, and deposited on something that swayed slightly beneath her feet.

'If you step back a little you'll feel the seat against your legs,' she heard him say through the clamour of her heartbeats, and still clutching at his shoulders, she did as she was told until she felt the edge of the seat pressing against the back of her calves, then, shakily but thankfully, she lowered herself on to it.

The boat seemed to rock precariously as he climbed into the seat beside her, but she held herself rigid, not wanting to show her nervous anxiety, then he said with that familiar smile in his voice, 'That wasn't so bad, was it?'

Roxy's stomach felt as if it had lodged somewhere in her throat, but she shook her head firmly and said: 'No—not too bad.'

'Right, then, let's go.' The engine roared to life, vibrating beneath her, then Marcus was steering the boat out on to the dam. The lifting, swaying motion of the boat made her feel a little sick at first, but she tried to relax, and moved her body with the sway, instead of against it, then a hand touched her arm. 'Are you all right?'

'I think so, yes,' she nodded.

'Shall I go a bit faster?'

'If you like.' She gritted her teeth as she felt the engine roaring ahead at full throttle, forcing her back against her seat, then she forgot everything except the feel of the sun and the wind, and the spray of the water on her face. She felt free, unchained, and curiously alive. 'This is fantastic!' she exclaimed loudly above the noise of the engine. 'I can remember once on the Kariba Lake when——'

'When what?' he questioned loudly when she came to an abrupt halt.

'It doesn't matter,' she shouted back, shutting her mind to the memory of that last occasion they had been together as a family; her father, her mother, and herself, in a boat on the Kariba Lake, laughing, happy, and unaware that tragedy was but a few days away.

'I know a place just up ahead where it's shady and private,' Marcus interrupted her mental vision of that hot, cloudless day so many years ago, and a few minutes later the engine slowed, then ceased abruptly.

The silent warmth of the veld was about them while Marcus tied up the boat and lifted her out on to a wooden platform similar to the one she had been on before. Later, seated on a rug beneath a shady tree, the memory of that afternoon on the lake returned to haunt her, and with it came the memory of that day when the world had seemed to explode about her.

'How did it happen?' Marcus asked, almost as if he had guessed her thoughts, and somehow she could not prevent the words from spilling from her lips.

'My mother and I were returning to Bulawayo after spending a few days with friends on a farm. A hand-grenade was thrown at the car, and my mother was killed instantly. I'd been lying in the back, reading a book, and all I could remember, before I woke up in hospital, was that terrific explosion and a blinding pain in my head.'

'Shrapnel,' said Marcus, grasping the situation.

'Daddy couldn't stay on in Rhodesia after that, and we came to South Africa. We settled in Johannesburg, but I went to the school for the blind at Worcester.' Why she was telling him all this, she did not know, but she felt oddly relieved at having shared the memory with him, and she smiled a little warily as she added: 'Now you know everything there is to know about me.'

'Not everything,' he contradicted, and suddenly she felt him close beside her on the rug. 'Take off your glasses.'

Roxy felt slightly taken aback at first, and then,

slowly, she removed the dark glasses and lowered them on to her lap. She had never before considered them as something behind which to hide, but at that moment she felt peculiarly vulnerable without them.

'I had a feeling your eyes would be green,' he said at last.

'Did you?' she asked with affected casualness, turning her face away from the touch of his fingers against the tiny scar above her left temple.

'Don't do that!' he ordered sharply, his hand staying hers as she was about to push the glasses back on to her nose. 'Never again do you wear those glasses when you're with me.'

'Never again?' A tight smile curved her mouth. 'You sound as though you intend to spend a lot of time with me in future.'

'Would you object to that?'

'I might,' she said, conscious of those strong fingers curled about her wrist, and sensing an undercurrent of anger in his voice and manner.

'Why?' he demanded bluntly.

'I have my reasons.'

His fingers tightened about her wrist. 'Don't be vague with me, Roxy. Come right out with it and tell me what it is you might object to.'

She felt trapped, but if he wanted the truth then he would get it. 'I don't want to become seriously involved.'

There was a tense little silence, then he demanded harshly, 'With me in particular, or are you generalising?'

'I was referring to men in general,' she replied tritely, easing her hand from his clasp, and he released her instantly.

'Do men repel you?'

'For heaven's sake!'

'I take it the answer to my question is no, men do not repel you, so the only conclusion I can come to is that you suffer from that crazy notion that you might become a burden to the man you're with.'

He had hit the target so accurately that it was some time before she could speak. 'Is it such a crazy notion?' she asked.

She felt him move angrily beside her. 'Let me decide that for myself, will you?' he echoed her father's words the previous evening.

'I don't think I could let you do that,' she argued softly.

A tense, drawn-out silence settled between them, then she heard him sigh. 'I'm not asking for much. Let's just take each day as it comes, and time will tell.' His hand was in her hair, his fingers against her scalp sending little shivers down her spine. 'I don't want to hurt you, Roxy. Before that happens I'll get out of your life—if that's what you want.'

She sat perfectly still, trying to analyse the feelings that stirred within her, then she asked a little huskily, 'What kind of man are you?'

'A very ordinary man, and a very hungry man at the moment,' he laughed shortly, moving away from her and allowing her to breathe easier. 'Shall we eat?'

'Yes, please.'

'What have we here?' he asked lightly, and she heard him delving into a basket. 'Chicken, tomatoes, bread rolls, cheese and biscuits, two glasses, and . . .' he laughed again, 'champagne.'

'Champagne?' she questioned incredulously. 'I don't believe you!'

'Listen,' he said, and there was a rustle of paper,

followed shortly afterwards by the sound of a cork popping from the neck of the bottle.

'It *is* champagne,' she exclaimed laughingly. 'What are we celebrating?'

'Who cares?' he shrugged casually, placing a glass in her hand. 'Let's drink to the future.'

'To the future,' she echoed, the bubbles tickling her nose as she raised the glass to her lips.

Roxy had long since overcome her embarrassment at eating in front of strangers, but she had a feeling that it was of no interest to Marcus how she managed to get her food to her mouth without fumbling, and she felt suddenly extraordinarily at ease with him as they ate their lunch in silence, and indulged in a second glass of champagne.

'What are you thinking about?' he asked suddenly when they had dispensed with the remnants of their lunch.

She smiled and plucked at the blade of grass she had found beneath her hand. 'I was thinking that I've told you so much about myself, one way or another, but I still know so little about you.'

'What would you like to know?'

'Tell me what you look like.'

'I've told you that already. I have three eyes, and a——'

'Oh, Marcus, be serious,' she laughed. 'What colour is your hair?'

'Light brown—almost fair, I suppose.'

'And your eyes?'

'Blue.'

'And you're tall—I've realised that,' she said, trying to visualise him, but not quite succeeding.

'I'm over six feet tall,' he admitted.

They lapsed into silence, and suddenly there seemed

to be nothing more to say. She fingered the dial of her watch nervously. Three o'clock. It was later than she had imagined.

'Isn't it time we packed up and left?' she suggested hesitantly, thinking of the long drive back to Johannesburg.

'You're bored,' he said, sounding accusing.

'No!' she protested hastily. 'Oh, no, please don't think that.'

'Then what's the hurry?'

'I—I thought perhaps *you* were bored,' she answered lamely, the blade of grass snapping between her fingers.

'You're lying,' he said sharply. 'You've suddenly become afraid of me for some reason.'

'Don't be ridiculous,' she argued, but she could not deny to herself that she was picking up the most disturbing vibrations which seemed to be emanating from him.

'Don't lie to me, Roxy,' he commanded roughly, and all at once he was dangerously close to her. 'Tell me the truth,' he urged.

'I—I've never met anyone like you before,' she heard herself saying unsteadily, and could have kicked herself afterwards for admitting so much.

'What's so different about me?''

'I don't . . . know. I—I wish I could explain.'

'It's that something indefinable; that little spark that lights up when two people meet.' He did not touch her, and yet his voice was like a slow caress, touching her like a soft breath of air until she trembled. 'You feel it too, don't you.'

'Marcus . . .' She felt confused and bewildered, and suddenly knew a desperate desire to see him more clearly in her mind. 'Would you let me see you—my way, I mean?' she voiced the request before she could prevent herself.

'I thought you'd never ask,' he laughed softly and, taking her hands in his, raised them to his face.

Her sensitive fingers touched the short, crisp hair, explored the broad forehead, the straight, heavy eyebrows, and lingered for a moment on his closed eyelids before trailing across the clearly defined cheekbones. His face was lean, the skin almost leathery, and the strong jaw ended in a square, determined chin. Her fingers trembled when they encountered his mouth, and the lower lip, slightly fuller than the top, moved against her fingers as if in a kiss, making her withdraw her hands at once.

'Well?' he demanded, and the hint of mockery in his voice sent a flow of warmth into her cheeks.

'You—you have strong features,' she stammered selfconsciously.

'A pleasing face, would you say?' he questioned with laughter in that deep, disturbing voice.

'Very pleasing, I think,' she acknowledged a little stiffly. 'But your mirror should tell you that.'

He drew a sharp, almost angry breath, then his hand was in her hair, fastening on to the nape of her neck as he warned thickly, 'Roxy, I'm going to kiss you.'

Startled into silence, she felt a peculiar weakness invade her body as he bore her backwards on to the rug. His breath mingled with hers, then her lips were being forced apart by the pressure of his mouth. She had been kissed before, but never with such a soul-searching intimacy that made every nerve in her body come alive in a throbbing response. His arms held her lightly but firmly despite her struggles, and when he finally released her her heart was beating so fast that she could hardly breathe.

'Don't do that again,' she said as she sat up and brushed her hair out of her face.

She was angry now, but her anger was directed at herself, and not at Marcus. Not surprisingly, however, he misunderstood her, and his voice was coldly controlled when he said: 'You were right. It's time I took you home.'

CHAPTER THREE

ROXY could not explain it to herself, but she felt chilled despite the warmth of the sun beating down on to her face and arms as she sat silently beside Marcus in the motorboat cleaving its way back to where they had started from earlier that day. He was angry; she had felt it in his touch when he had helped her into the boat, and she felt it again now as he lifted her on to the wooden platform, and it left her feeling tense and uncomfortable, wishing she could offer him a reasonable explanation, but unable to find the right words.

'Roxy!' A light, faintly petulant voice interrupted her turbulent thoughts. 'Well, fancy meeting you here of all places!'

Recognition ignited a deep-seated irritation in Roxy and she said stiffly, 'Hello, Vera.'

'Aren't you going to introduce me to your friend?' that petulant voice demanded, and Roxy sighed inwardly. She had problems enough without Vera making it worse, she told herself, but she made the introductions nevertheless.

'Marcus, this is Vera Sinclair. Vera . . . Marcus Fleming.'

'How do you do, Miss Sinclair,' Marcus said quietly.

'Oh, please don't be so formal, Mårcus,' Vera insisted with a hint of seductive laughter in her voice. 'Roxy and I have been friends and neighbours for years, so we're sure to meet again.'

'No doubt we *shall* meet again,' Marcus replied, and he, too, sounded as if he were smiling.

Impatient voices called to Vera from across the parking area, and she sighed, saying with obvious reluctance, 'Oh well . . . be seeing you, and soon, I hope.'

There was an excited clamour of voices mingling with loud laughter, then a car's engine was being revved with unnecessary violence before it was driven away at speed with the sound of gravel scattering beneath the spinning wheels.

'She's a friend of yours?' Marcus asked Roxy some minutes later when they were driving back to Johannesburg.

'I wouldn't exactly call her a friend,' Roxy replied almost defensively. 'We've known each other since my father and I moved in next door to them, but we have very little in common except for the fact that her mother does quite a lot of charity work for the blind.'

'So you can't exactly tell Vera to get the hell out of your life,' he remarked dryly, obviously sensing her dislike.

'I'm under no obligation to her,' Roxy said tritely, and they lapsed once again into that stony silence which lasted until they had arrived at her home.

She felt guilty about her behaviour now as he accompanied her to the door, and she was desperate suddenly to ease the tension between them.

'Marcus, I——'

'I won't come in, if you don't mind,' he interrupted the hesitant beginnings of her invitation, releasing her arm at the same time. 'I'll call you some time.'

She tried to say something, but couldn't, and moments later a car door slammed before it was driven swiftly from the house. 'I'll call you some time,' he had said, but Roxy had a sinking feeling that it would be some time *never*. She sighed as she went inside, and decided that this was just another chapter in her life which she would have to write off as an unfortunate experience.

She was not surprised when Vera put in an appearance early the following morning. Her interest in Marcus had been only too obvious, and Roxy smiled inwardly with a touch of cynicism when quick, light footsteps entered the small room downstairs which she had turned into a workroom for herself.

'Hello, Roxy. It's me—Vera. I just had to come and see you this morning.'

'Oh?' Roxy remarked, feigning innocence as she sat back in her chair and placed a soothing hand on Sheba's bristling back.

Sheba had never taken to Vera, and her low growl had warned Roxy of Vera's arrival long before she herself had identified those light steps.

'Where on earth did you meet that gorgeous hunk of man you were with yesterday?'

There it was; direct and to the point, and so typical of Vera Sinclair, Roxy thought.

'Is he gorgeous?' she asked, her innocence tinged with curiosity.

'Oh, Roxy, if only you could *see* him!' Vera exclaimed with an ecstatic sigh, and then she drew a sharp, uncomfortable breath. 'Sorry ... that was clumsy of me.'

'For heaven's sake, Vera,' Roxy said irritably. 'I'm well past the stage of being touchy about remarks like that, and you know it.'

'Yes, of course.' There was the scrape of a chair on

the floor as Vera got to her feet. 'Oh, well, I just thought I'd let you know. If you ever get tired of Marcus Fleming, toss him my way, darling.'

A tinkling, almost inane laugh filled the small room, and then Vera's heels were clicking across the floor and growing fainter down the passage and into the hall until the front door closed behind her.

Roxy expelled the air from her lungs, then, for some inexplicable reason, she was laughing, and she was laughing still when Maggie brought in her tea.

'What did Miss Vera want?' Maggie asked suspiciously.

'She wanted to know more about Marcus Fleming,' Roxy replied, trying to stifle her laugh behind her hand.

'That Mr Fleming——'

'I know,' Roxy interrupted humorously. 'He's a gorgeous hunk of man.'

'Who told you that?' Maggie demanded sharply.

'Vera,' Roxy laughed. 'She was quite ecstatic about his looks.'

'Are you going to see him again?'

Roxy sobered at once and stirred the tea Maggie had placed on the desk in front of her. 'I don't think so.'

'That would be a pity, Miss Roxy.'

Maggie left the room without explaining her statement, and Roxy was left feeling curiously deflated.

Roxy had little time during that week, and the following, to think much about herself, or Marcus Fleming. Chris Thompson was making a rapid recovery, and she found herself dividing her time at the clinic between him and several other patients, often snatching a light meal at the clinic and remaining until Basil could give her a lift home.

The pressure fortunately eased off towards the end of the second week, and she was in her workroom one morning when Sheba's excited bark interrupted her work. She switched off the tape recorder and removed her earphones.

'Sheba?' she questioned, wondering whether Sheba had decided it was time to go for a walk, then she sensed someone else's presence in the room with her and asked warily, 'Who is there?'

'Marcus,' came the abrupt reply. 'Am I welcome?'

'Yes, of course,' she said quickly, her heart leaping wildly in her breast as he crossed the room and pulled a chair up close to her own.

'It seems to me we parted company on a sour note a few weeks ago.'

'It was my fault,' she admitted apologetically.

'I seem to remember it was mine for taking unwanted liberties,' he corrected, and there was the warmth of a smile in his voice.

'Marcus . . .' She extended her hands towards him in a silent gesture of appeal, and a warmth rushed into her heart, lifting the corners of her mouth in a smile when those strong fingers clasped hers.

'I rushed the fences a little,' he said softly. 'Will you allow me a re-take if I promise to take it slow?'

Her smile broadened and, in reply, she asked: 'Will you stay and have tea with me?'

'If you'll have dinner with me this evening,' he countered swiftly.

'I'm afraid I can't,' she declined, her heart sinking. 'I promised a little boy at the clinic I'd visit him this evening, and I can't let him down.'

'Then I'll take you there, and we'll have dinner afterwards,' he offered without hesitation, but Roxy felt disinclined to accept his kind offer after the way she had treated him before.

'I couldn't impose on you in that way,' she said simply, and the hands which held hers were instantly withdrawn.

'Why don't you just tell me you don't want to have dinner with me, and forget the excuses?' he demanded harshly, and the waves of anger emanating from him made her shrink inwardly.

'That isn't what I——'

'Hello there!' a light voice interrupted Roxy's explanation. 'Anyone home?'

'In here, Vera,' Roxy called back disconsolately, a staying hand going at once to the agitated Sheba's collar.

'I just dropped in for a moment to——' Her footsteps halted just within the door, and that familiar tinkling laugh tripped off her lips. 'My goodness, I wondered whose Lamborghini was parked in the drive, and it must be yours, of course, Marcus.'

Marcus rose to his feet. 'Good morning, Vera.'

There was a brief silence during which Roxy sensed they were summing each other up, and then Maggie's footsteps could be heard entering the room. 'Tea, Miss Roxy.'

'Thank you, Maggie.'

'Shall I pour, darling?' Vera offered the moment Maggie had left, and Roxy nodded slightly.

'Please do.'

Vera was in her element, naturally, playing hostess, and she talked incessantly during the next half hour, engaging Marcus in conversation almost to the exclusion of Roxy, then, after a slight pause, she asked casually, 'By the way, what were you both looking so serious about when I walked in earlier?'

There was an uncomfortable little silence, then

Marcus replied in a clipped voice, 'I was trying to persuade Roxy to have dinner with me this evening.'

'Oh, Roxy has this thing about eating out, and she's always been a bit of a stick-in-the-mud,' Vera told him unkindly and untruthfully and, before Roxy could protest, she added with a beguiling laugh, 'If you need a stand-in, just remember that I live next door.'

'Would you have dinner with me this evening, then?' Marcus's request surprised Roxy into abject silence.

'Just you try and stop me!' Vera laughed without hesitation.

'Very well, I'll call for you at seven—and now I must be on my way.' Marcus stood up and crossed the floor towards the door. 'Thanks for the tea, Roxy.'

'I must be going as well, so I'll come out with you, Marcus,' Vera said hastily, her heels clicking swiftly across the floor. 'Cheerio, Roxy. See you some time.'

Roxy sat there behind her desk as if turned to stone while she listened to their footsteps growing fainter down the passage. She was stunned, incredulous, and deep down inside her there was a stab of pain that made her frown with angry irritation. What did she care about Marcus Fleming? He could do as he pleased, and was not answerable to her for his behaviour. She got to her feet agitatedly, stumbled over the chair Marcus had carelessly left in her path, and then, stupidly, she knelt down on the floor and cried as if she were a child and someone had run off with her pet toy.

She went to the clinic that afternoon, and again that evening to see Chris, but she found it difficult trying to concentrate on their conversation while her mind was busy thinking of Marcus and Vera together, enjoying a meal somewhere which had initially been intended for her.

'Oh, damn!' she muttered when she eventually left Chris's ward. 'Pull yourself together, Roxana Cunningham. You're becoming obsessed with Marcus Fleming, and that's the worst thing you could ever do.'

'Hello, what's up?' Basil asked laughingly, taking her arm and falling into step beside her. 'I've never known you to talk to yourself before?'

She smiled reluctantly. 'I must be getting old.'

'Nonsense!' he retorted. 'What you need is a strong cup of tea before I drive you home.'

On their way to his office he ordered a tray of tea, and when it was eventually brought to them he poured and handed her a cup. Under the influence of Basil's charming company and the strong cup of tea, Roxy found herself relaxing and forgetting temporarily about Marcus and Vera while she laughed with him as he passed on some of his patients' funny anecdotes.

Her father was still up when Roxy arrived at the house an hour later and, for the first time in some years, she refused the glass of wine he offered her and went straight up to her room, leaving a baffled Theodore behind in the living-room.

'You sound pretty,' Chris said the following afternoon when she sat talking to him on the lawn in the gardens of the clinic. 'I wish I could see you.'

Roxy smiled to herself. 'You could always see me with your hands.'

'How?'

'Like this,' she said and, finding his hands, she raised them to her face. 'Explore my face with your fingertips. Go on, don't be shy.'

Small, cool fingers trailed hesitantly across her features, and finally came to rest against her lips. 'Are you smiling?' he asked uncertainly.

Roxy's smile broadened as she murmured, 'Yes, I am.'

'Your skin is soft,' he announced, trailing his fingers across her cheeks once more, then she felt him lean closer to sniff at her lightly. 'And you always smell so nice.'

'You're getting very clever at being blind,' she laughed softly.

'It's funny, but——' Chris paused, removing his hands from her face.

'What's funny?' she prompted when the silence lengthened between them.

The child sighed and laughed a little selfconsciously. 'When I'm with you, Roxy, I'm not scared any more.'

Roxy's heart warmed to him. 'There's never any need to be afraid, Chris. No matter who you're with.'

'My bandages are coming off tomorrow,' he said eventually, and some of his anxiety was transferred to her. 'I don't think I'll mind so much any more if I never see again, but ... will you be here when Dr Vaughn takes them off?'

'If you want me to, I will.'

There was the rustle of a starched uniform, then the nursing Sister's authoritative voice said: 'It's getting chilly out, Chris, and it's almost time for Dr Vaughn's visit.'

Chris sighed, but said goodbye to Sheba and rose obediently to his feet. 'You'll be here tomorrow, Roxy? Promise?'

'I'll be here, Chris, and that's a promise,' she replied calmly. 'Go along with the Sister now.'

The sound of the starched uniform grew fainter, then Roxy placed an arm about Sheba's neck and said tiredly, 'It's time we went home too, Sheba.'

'Want a lift?' a deep, familiar voice asked directly behind her, and Roxy's nerves coiled into a knot at the pit of her stomach as she rose slowly to her feet and turned towards him.

'Marcus?' she murmured his name questioningly.

'At your service.'

She suddenly felt incredibly nervous as she said: 'Maggie will be here to fetch me any minute now.'

'No, she won't,' Marcus contradicted. 'I telephoned the house and told her I'd be collecting you.'

She felt confused, bewildered, and the strained silence did nothing to relieve her tension. 'Why are you here?' she finally asked.

'I've been invited to dinner, and your father tells me you play an excellent game of chess,' he said, confusing her more, then his hand was on her arm, sending those little shivers of awareness through her. 'My car is this way.'

They walked across the lawn in silence towards the car park, and Roxy was assisted into the front seat. Sheba willingly climbed into the back, then Marcus walked round to the other side and climbed in beside Roxy.

'Well?' he demanded harshly, slamming the door behind him, but not starting the car. 'Why don't you say what's on your mind?'

There were several things she could have said, but suddenly they seemed childish and quite unnecessary. 'I have nothing to say,' she told him warily.

'Well, I have plenty to say to you,' he exploded with a violence that made her shrink back against the door. 'Firstly ... when I asked you to come out with me yesterday, it was because I desired your company, and I wouldn't have offered to bring you here to the clinic if I'd considered it an inconvenience. Secondly ... I took Vera up on her suggestion that she'd act as a stand-in because I was so damnably angry with you that I wanted to hurt you in some way. Thirdly ...

someone really ought to tell that young lady that, even in this permissive age, men still prefer to do the running. And lastly . . .' he drew a sharp, angry breath that made her wince inwardly, 'take those damn glasses off when you're with me so I can see your eyes!'

They were removed roughly from her face as he spoke, and suddenly her vulnerability made her resort to anger. 'You have no right to speak to me like this,' she accused coldly. 'You chose to misunderstand me yesterday, but that's beside the point. Whom you choose to spend your time with is also entirely your own affair, and I would prefer it if, after this evening, we don't meet again.'

'Right!' Marcus said sharply, thrusting her glasses back on to her face. 'Then we understand each other at last!'

Sheba whined softly in the back of the car, sensing something in the atmosphere, then she, too, fell silent as Marcus started the car and drove away from the clinic.

During the drive out to Houghton the antagonistic atmosphere between them became almost explosive, and Roxy was ridiculously close to tears when he finally parked his car in front of her home. She could not spend the rest of the evening in his company with this tension between them, and when he switched off the engine she turned in her seat towards him.

They started speaking simultaneously, broke off abruptly, tried again, and finally gave up when they were reduced to laughter.

'Do we call a truce?' he asked at last.

'Yes . . . please,' she whispered, relief choking her.

He removed her glasses gently this time, drawing a sharp breath when he saw the tears brimming her eyes, and then she found herself in his arms with her head being pressed into his shoulder. His masculine cologne was in her nostrils while his warm breath fanned her cheek, and suddenly it seemed so right to be there close against him.

'I'm a cad! I know it!' he grunted, stroking her hair away from her face. 'Let's try again, shall we?'

She nodded, her throat too tight to speak, and they sat like that for some time until Sheba whined impatiently and tried to push her nose between them.

They laughed as they drew apart, then Marcus remarked with mock sadness in his voice, 'Ah, Sheba, you've just ruined a beautiful moment.'

Sheba whined and barked in response as if she had understood, and Roxy reached over to the back to stroke her.

'Don't worry, Sheba,' she laughed happily. 'Marcus was only teasing you.'

The evening turned out to be pleasant and relaxing. After dinner her father brought out the chessboard and set it up on a low table between Marcus and Roxy, then he sat back, literally rubbing his hands together with satisfaction as Marcus set about beating Roxy at the game.

When Marcus finally announced that it was 'checkmate' Theodore exclaimed delightedly, and clapped his hands, but instead of being embarrassed, Roxy felt oddly pleased that Marcus had won.

Theodore poured wine and they talked for some time until he was called out unexpectedly to a client, then Roxy found herself alone with Marcus, and she was inexplicably nervous for some reason.

She sensed more than heard him approach her chair, then her hands were taken and she was drawn to her feet.

'I was watching you while we had dinner this evening,' he said, ushering her towards the sofa and seating himself beside her. 'Was Vera telling the truth? Do you feel embarrassed about eating in public?'

A slow smile curved her mouth. 'I've been blind for ten years, Marcus. I think I've mastered the art of eating without embarrassing those who are with me, don't you?'

'I agree entirely, but Vera said——'

'She was having fun at my expense,' Roxy interrupted a little bitterly.

His fingers tightened about hers. 'Do I take it then that you'll dine out with me one evening soon?'

'If you feel inclined to ask me again, yes.'

'Tomorrow evening?'

'Isn't that a bit too soon?' she teased, but when he remained silent, she added hastily, 'Please, I'm not trying to find excuses.'

'If tomorrow is too soon, then what about Saturday evening?' he suggested, and Roxy could find no reason to refuse.

'I'd like that,' she replied, conscious of a hard thigh against her own.

'Seven o'clock?'

'Yes.'

They talked quietly after that, about the things he hoped to achieve in the business he had inherited from his uncle, and although her awareness of him grew, her nervousness evaporated, and she felt strangely disappointed when he finally said goodnight and left.

She lay thinking about him for a long time that night, her desire not to become too deeply involved fighting against the strange attraction she felt for him. It was a dangerous attraction, and she knew instinctively that she could get hurt, but was it not worth the chance she was taking? Was it worth risking her peace of mind to become involved with a man like Marcus Fleming who could never endure being tied down to someone like herself? There were so many questions rushing through her mind, and for none of them could she find an answer. Perhaps the only solution would be to wait, and allow circumstances to develop in whatever direction they pleased.

Roxy slipped behind the screens in the children's ward of the clinic the following afternoon. Basil was there, and the ward Sister, but the young boy in the high bed had recognised her light step.

'Roxy?' he whispered anxiously.

'I'm here, Chris,' she assured him hastily.

'Hold my hand.'

She found his hand and held it tightly between her own as Basil proceeded to snip away at the bandages.

'Just relax, young fellow,' Basil warned when Chris began to fidget. 'We'll have these bandages off soon.'

'Where's my mum and dad?' Chris asked unexpectedly.

'They're waiting outside,' Basil told him. 'Do you want me to tell them to come in?'

'No,' Chris said a little anxiously. 'Not yet.'

'Right,' said Basil at length, and the scissors ceased their snipping. 'Open your eyes, Chris. Just take it easy, and don't expect too much at first.'

'It isn't so dark any more,' Chris announced excitedly, his fingers tightening about Roxy's. 'There's something moving. It's your hand. I can see it now, and it's getting clearer.'

'That's wonderful,' Basil laughed softly.

'Roxy, I can see!' Chris laughed, his young voice vibrating with excitement. 'I can see just a little, but I *can* see, and . . . oh, you're pretty!'

'Oh, Chris . . .' Roxy swallowed down the lump in her throat, 'I'm so happy for you.'

The ward Sister had called in Mr and Mrs Thompson, and in the excitement Roxy stepped aside and whispered to Basil, 'I'll wait out in the corridor.'

In the passage outside the ward Roxy leaned against the wall and unobtrusively brushed away her tears with the tips of her fingers. She was a fool to cry, but she was happy for Chris, and—yes, she had to admit it—more than a little envious. It would be cowardly to hide from the truth—her father had taught her that. 'Be honest with yourself,' he had told her once when she had rebelled against her blindness. 'When you admit your failings to yourself, then you can face them and conquer them.'

She was being honest with herself now. The old rebellion had stirred within her once again, but she had clamped down on it hastily. She envied Chris, but she was happy for him, and her happiness outweighed her envy at that moment. She did not wish upon the child those years of struggling to overcome the mental and physical obstacles caused by blindness. Independence was difficult to obtain, and even now she was not entirely independent.

Approaching footsteps interrupted her thoughts, and she recognised the ward Sister's voice inviting her to join her for tea in her office. It was there that Basil found her some minutes later.

'Chris's parents wanted to see you, but you'd vanished,' he told her, accepting a cup of tea from the Sister.

'I thought it best to leave them alone together,' Roxy smiled a little unsteadily.

'Chris is asking for you.'

She nodded slowly. 'I suppose he'll go home soon.'

'He's going home tomorrow.'

'I'll miss him,' she said sadly.

'Believe it or not,' Basil laughed, 'so will I.'

Roxy finished her tea and returned to the ward to see Chris for the last time. The screens had been removed from around his bed, and with Basil no longer there, the children were noisy with exuberance.

'Roxy,' said Chris as she approached his bed, 'I'm going home tomorrow.'

'I know.'

'Dr Vaughn says I'll have to wear glasses, but he thinks my eye will get stronger.'

'I'm sure it will.'

He was silent for a moment, and then she felt his small hand slipping into hers. 'I'm going to miss you, Roxy.'

She swallowed the rising lump in her throat and laughed with forced gaiety. 'No, you're not! You're going to return to school one of these days, and then you'll be with all your friends once more.'

'I won't forget you, and I won't forget Sheba,' he insisted with a certain stubbornness that was touching.

'It will be nice to be remembered,' she admitted eventually, fighting against the tears that threatened. 'Sheba and I won't forget you either.'

When Maggie drove Roxy home that afternoon, she did not question the tears that flowed from behind those dark glasses on to Roxy's cheeks, but she did produce a wad of tissues for the mopping-up process before they arrived at the house.

'It's never easy saying goodbye,' her father had once told her when he found her crying after saying farewell to a patient. 'But tomorrow there'll be someone else for you to worry about, and then the others will be forgotten to a certain extent.'

Wise words, Roxy realised, but Chris had somehow crept right into her heart, and she suspected it was going to take a little longer to forget him.

CHAPTER FOUR

THE band seemed to be playing loudly in order to be heard above the raised voices of the diners, and Roxy felt as though her head was about to split. She had looked forward to dining out with Marcus, but she had never imagined it would affect her in this way. Conversation was virtually impossible and, as the evening wore on, Roxy found it increasingly difficult to make the effort to speak. It felt as though she had been trapped in a rowdy madhouse, and she was becoming frantic with the desire for escape.

'Dance with me, Roxy,' Marcus suggested when they had had their meal, and drew her to her feet and on to the dance floor before she could protest.

'I'm afraid I'm not a very good dancer,' she warned nervously.

'Neither am I,' he laughed close to her ear. 'Let's settle for a slow shuffle around the floor.'

His arm was firm about her waist, drawing her unnervingly close to him, and somehow, as they moved across the floor in time to the music, she matched her steps to his. The noise was becoming deafening, and her tortured eardrums throbbed protestingly in time to the heavy beat of the bass drum. Marcus tightened his arm about her waist and she felt his chin brush against her temple, but not even the thrill of his nearness could eliminate what she was suffering at that moment.

'You've been very quiet this evening, Roxy,' he remarked when they finally returned to their table.

'I'm sorry.' What else could she say? she wondered miserably. If she tried to explain, would he understand, or would he consider that she was merely seeking an excuse to bring the evening to an end?

'Is something wrong?' he questioned her sharply, finding her hands across the table and gripping them tightly. 'You seem nervous and edgy.'

'No, no, there's nothing——'

'Roxy!' His voice was stern and commanding. 'The truth.'

The truth! Oh, God, she wanted to scream it at him, but she dared not. 'Forgive me, Marcus. The food has been excellent, but——'

'But?' he prompted tersely, and she knew that, whatever happened, she could no longer keep silent.

'It's the noise,' she said at last. 'You may not notice it, but it sounds to me as though there are a million voices trying to make themselves heard above the noise of the band, and——' She swallowed nervously. 'I'm sorry.'

'Come,' he said at once, drawing her to her feet and draping her coat about her shoulders. 'I'm taking you out of here.'

'Marcus . . .' she began hesitantly some minutes later when she was seated beside him in his car and being driven heaven knows where. 'I've spoiled the evening for you.'

'No, you haven't,' he said at once, and his hand clasped hers briefly in her lap. 'I'm taking you to Carlo's. It's quiet there, and he makes a good strong cup of coffee.'

Roxy said nothing, but she had never felt so miserable in her life before. She felt a freak and, worse still, she felt certain that Marcus considered her so.

Less than ten minutes later Roxy was being ushered into another restaurant where the voices of the diners were nothing but a pleasant murmur on the ears while recorded music offered a soothing and relaxing background.

'Ah, Carlo,' Marcus exclaimed moments after they had entered, and a spate of Italian followed that left Roxy feeling lost and bewildered before Marcus drew her more firmly to his side and said: 'Carlo, I'd like you to meet Miss Roxana Cunningham. Roxy, this is my good friend Carlo.'

'How do you do, Carlo,' she smiled forcibly, extending her hand and, to her surprise, she felt the man's lips brushing against her fingers.

'I am honoured to meet you, Signorina Cunningham,' he said in his heavily accented English.

'I told Roxy you make an excellent cup of coffee, Carlo.'

'The very best,' Carlo agreed delightedly, releasing her hand. 'Sit down, and I will bring it at once, Signor Marcus.'

Marcus's arm about her shoulders guided her towards a table, and when she was seated he asked: 'Is this better?'

'Much better,' she replied with a rueful smile. 'Marcus, I'm sorry.'

'Don't say that again,' he ordered firmly. 'It was crassly inconsiderate of me not to have realised that the noise might affect you in that way—and to tell the truth, I prefer the peace and quiet of Carlo's restaurant.'

'You're just saying that to make me feel better,' she accused.

'Roxy, don't be infuriating.'

'Infuriating?' she echoed curiously. 'In what way?'

'Don't you trust me?'

Roxy considered this for a moment. 'Should I?'

'That's a good question,' he laughed, grasping the ulterior meaning behind her words, and she coloured at her own audacity.

'Your coffee, *signore*, *signorina*,' Carlo interrupted their conversation.

'Thank you, Carlo,' Marcus replied, then they were left alone once more.

Roxy sugared her coffee and sipped at the aromatic brew. 'Hm, this *is* good.'

'Tell me about your work at the clinic,' Marcus prompted. 'You were talking to a little boy in the clinic gardens the other day.'

'That was little Chris Thompson,' she explained. 'There was a possibility that he might be totally blind, but fortunately he's maintained the vision of one eye.' There was a hint of sadness in her voice as she added: 'He went home yesterday.'

'And you, Roxy?' Marcus questioned her directly. 'Is there no hope of——'

'No hope at all,' she interrupted, shrinking mentally from this topic of conversation.

'There's an eye surgeon in Vienna who's been performing absolute miracles during the past few years.'

'Marcus, the optic nerves have been severed, and no operation in the world could rectify that. Besides . . .' she drew a careful breath, 'Basil Vaughn is the best eye specialist in the country, and also the most brilliant surgeon. He's called in more than a dozen eye surgeons to review my case, and they've all said it's hopeless. I've accepted the fact that I'm going to be blind for the rest of my life, and I don't want my hopes raised again.'

Marcus was silent for a moment, and she was beginning to suspect that she had displeased him when he said: 'To look at you one would never say you're blind.'

'I'm normal, except for my sight, and I have a place in society just like everyone else. I don't want to be pampered, or treated any differently.' She smiled suddenly. 'My father and I have a very good understanding. We always tell each other the truth, no matter how much it may hurt, and in that way I know I'm not being deceived or cheated.'

'Do people try to deceive you?'

'Mostly I find they try to cheat me into buying something ridiculous when I go shopping,' she laughed shortly.

'Can you tell when they do?'

'Nearly always, yes, but I seldom buy anything in the clothing line unless Maggie is with me.' They drank their coffee in silence, and when she eventually pushed her empty cup aside, she said: 'Let's talk about you for a change. Do you live in a house or a flat?'

'A flat,' he replied in an abrupt fashion, and she suspected that he disliked being questioned.

'Who does the cooking and cleaning for you?'

'The flat is serviced. I occasionally rustle up something for myself, but most of the time I eat out.'

'With a different woman each night for company?' she teased lightly.

'Yes,' he agreed, and she sensed the smile in his voice. 'I have this little black book, you see, with all their names, addresses, and statistics, and the one I select depends entirely on what mood I happen to be in.'

'What mood are you in this evening?' she questioned humorously. 'A charitable, sympathetic, feeling-sorry-for-her mood?'

'I don't feel sorry for you, Roxy.' The smile had left his voice. 'You're attractive, and you're different.'

Roxy stiffened. 'By different, I presume you mean blind.'

'Different in yourself, you prickly hedgehog,' he scolded harshly, capturing her hands across the table, and sending that familiar current of awareness rippling through her. 'There are other reasons why I enjoy your company, but I'll tell you those reasons some other time.'

The atmosphere had suddenly become intimate, and much too dangerous. 'You make me nervous,' she said quietly.

'Do I?'

She tilted her head slightly as if she were trying to make up her mind about something, then she said accusingly, 'You're laughing at me.'

'Not at you,' he corrected, his thumbs moving in a sensual caress across the backs of her hands. 'I'm laughing at myself.'

'At yourself?' she frowned.

'If you'd been any other girl, Roxy, you may have had reason to feel nervous. Our relationship has reached the stage where I usually do my level best to persuade my companion into my bed.'

'Oh,' she said dully, her colour deepening, then receding. She was not quite sure what she had expected, but his explanation had somehow extinguished a light within her.

'Does that shock you?' he questioned softly.

'Not really.'

'Does it surprise you, then, that I haven't tried to

seduce you?' he persisted, unaware of the pain his probing questions were arousing.

'No,' she said stiffly, removing her hands firmly from his. 'My blindness usually places a damper on a man's natural desires.'

'My God, Roxy! You're no less a woman because you're blind!' His voice seemed to vibrate with incredulous anger, and when she did not answer him, he said roughly, 'Come on, it's time I took you home.'

Roxy sat tense and silent beside him in the car as he drove through the streets of the city and out to Houghton. The evening had been a failure; *she* was a failure, and perhaps, she thought bitterly, it had been foolish of her to think she could be like other women. No man could truly be interested in a girl who is blind, so why should she feel hurt about the things Marcus had said?

The car slowed down, the tires crunching on the gravel driveway, and then it stopped. Marcus switched off the engine, and in the ensuing silence Roxy's shaking fingers sought the catch on the door.

'Wait!' He leaned across her, his hand staying hers, and her pulse quickened as she felt his breath fanning her cheek. 'Don't be under a misapprehension, Roxy,' he said, and that deep, velvety voice was like a slow caress stirring her senses. 'You're *very* desirable, but your innocence was obvious to me in the way you reacted that day at the dam when I kissed you. You were frightened, I know that now, and I don't want to frighten you again.'

He sounded convincing and, in her desperate desire to believe him, she whispered daringly, 'I'm not frightened now.'

He was silent for one awful moment, then he asked with a hint of humour in his voice, 'Are you asking me to seduce you?'

'I'm asking you to treat me like a woman,' she answered, his nearness making her behave in a way she had never dared to do before.

'Haven't I been trying to do that since the first time we met?'

'You have,' she admitted truthfully, 'but I wasn't prepared for what followed.'

'And you're prepared for it now?'

Roxy had a feeling that she was treading on dangerous ground, and that her answer would determine her future in no uncertain terms. *Was* she prepared for it, or was she blundering into something she would find herself unable to cope with eventually? She sensed the tension in Marcus as he waited for her to reply, and she stammered nervously, 'I—I think so.'

'Then let's find out, shall we?' he laughed softly, drawing her towards him.

She remained passive and uncertain in his arms, but when his lips found hers and coaxed them apart, she melted against him and kissed him back with more warmth than she had intended. His kiss was gentle this time, but with an underlying sensuality that awakened dormant emotions she had not known she possessed and, when that hand beneath her coat moved upwards from her waist to her breast, she trembled and drew closer to him instinctively.

Marcus released her with unexpected suddenness and, with his arms no longer about her, she shivered and asked anxiously, 'Did I do something wrong?'

'I don't intend to rush you, Roxy,' he said in an odd voice as he raised her hand to his lips. 'I'm going to take you inside now.'

Roxy felt strangely disappointed as she walked up the steps with him to the front door. What had she expected? she wondered confusedly as she pulled her coat closer about her to shut out the cold night air.

'Shall I put on the light?' he asked when they stood in the hall, and her whispered 'no' was barely spoken before his arms slid inside her coat to encircle her waist and draw her towards him until her slenderness came to rest against the hard length of him.

She felt again that current of electricity flowing through her, then he was kissing her with that passionate intensity she had known once before, but this time she did not withdraw from him. Her arms went up about his neck, and she surrendered herself to the wild, throbbing emotions that stormed through her body.

His hands were hard against her back, and her breasts were hurting against his chest, but she did not care. She wanted this moment to go on and on for ever, but Marcus moved against her without warning, removing her arms from about his neck, and putting her aside.

'I must go,' he said in a strangely hoarse voice, 'but I'll see you tomorrow.'

His lips brushed hers very briefly, then he was gone, leaving her in the silent, darkened hall with a heart that was beating alarmingly fast in her breast.

She had never felt like this before; so elated, so very much a woman. She had a vague suspicion as to what was happening to her, but she could not put a name to it—not yet—not until she was sure of herself, and of Marcus.

'Marcus,' she whispered his name aloud as she went up to her room. His name was like a melody in her heart and, foolishly perhaps, she allowed herself to dream that night of the things she had always shut so firmly out of her life.

The following two weeks were deliriously happy weeks for Roxy. Marcus occupied almost every free moment she had, but she did not object. He took her to Carlo's for dinner on several occasions, and escorted her once to the music festival in the City Hall, but he also spent quite a few evenings at her home with her father and herself, which made her suspect that he enjoyed proving to her that he could still outwit her at chess whenever it pleased him.

Roxy's awakening came at the housewarming party of friends of his, when her sensitive ears picked up a conversation between Marcus and their host.

'Attractive girl you brought with you this evening,' David Whitby was saying. 'Pity she's blind, though.'

'Roxy doesn't need to be pitied,' came Marcus's reply.

'Are you serious about her?'

'You know me, Dave,' Marcus laughed shortly. 'I like variety.'

Roxy's insides began to shake. Was she merely one of the variety that added spice to his life? It was an unpalatable thought she did not linger on as she heard David Whitby speaking once more.

'It's time you got yourself married, and settled down, Marcus,' he said. 'You're not getting any younger, you know.'

'If I ever decide to plunge myself into the state of matrimony it will have to be to someone who could share my interests,' Marcus replied testily.

'Do you have someone in mind?'

If Marcus replied to that, then his reply was drowned out by the shrill laughter of the women seated beside Roxy, but she had heard enough to make her realise that she had lived in a fool's paradise over the past weeks.

The remainder of the evening dragged for Roxy

and, when they finally left the party, she was so tense that she could hardly speak. All she could think of while Marcus drove her home were his remarks about liking variety, and not marrying anyone unless this person could share his interests. What was that formidable list of interests her father had rattled off to her one evening? Karate, squash, mountaineering and yachting, she recalled them one by one, and it was like driving a sword repeatedly into her very soul. Marriage to Marcus had not entered her thoughts as yet, and now there was less chance of it ever doing so. She could never share in those interesting activities even if she had wanted to, so there was no purpose in continuing with a relationship which would eventually become distasteful to both of them, she decided bitterly.

'Do I get invited to stay for something to drink?' Marcus asked lightly when he had unlocked the front door for her and stood aside for her to enter.

'No, it's late, and I—I'm rather tired,' she apologised haltingly, knowing she could not bear him near her now that she had so much to think about.

'I'll see you tomorrow evening, then.'

'I don't think so, Marcus. I have so much work to catch up on.'

'I'll give you a ring at any rate,' he announced, drawing her into a swift embrace and kissing her hard on the mouth. 'Goodnight, Roxy.'

She heard his car go down the drive a few minutes later, and only then did she lock the door and go upstairs to her room. It was not too late to forget him, she told herself as she undressed herself and climbed into bed, but while she lay there waiting for sleep to overtake her she realised with painful certainty that it *was* too late already. Marcus had shattered her defences at their very first meeting, and later he had stripped her of her final layer of protection; her determination to exclude men from her life. She was left now with the despairing knowledge that she had fallen in love with a man who cared as little for her, apparently, as he had cared for any of the women he had known in his past.

There were no tears, no silent recriminations, only a quiet acceptance, and a firm decision to keep out of his way in future in the hope that she might forget the dream of happiness she had nurtured for so brief a time.

When the telephone rang after dinner the following evening she knew instinctively that it would be Marcus, and she steeled herself when her father called her into the hall to take the call. Her hand was damp and shaking when she lifted the receiver to her ear, and the sound of his voice at the other end did nothing to placate the nervous tension that coiled through her. It merely made her more aware of the desperate and futile longings which churned within her for something she could not have.

'Have dinner with me tomorrow evening,' he suggested in his usual commanding manner, and although her heart longed to say 'yes', her mind told her that it would be a mistake.

'I'm afraid I can't,' she said, grasping at the first excuse she could think of. 'I'm going out with my father to spend the evening with friends of ours.'

'What about the evening after that, then?'

'Dr Vaughn is taking me to a party at his golf club.'

There was a brief, ominous silence during which she felt terrifyingly certain he must hear the heavy thudding of her heart, then he asked with a hint of that familiar smile in his voice, 'Are you giving me the brush-off, Roxy?'

'Oh, God, give me strength,' she prayed desperately, and then, her fingernails biting into her palm, she said untruthfully, 'N-no, of course not.'

The line seemed to crackle with silence once more, then he said abruptly, 'I'll see you some time, then.'

The line went dead before she could reply, and she stood there a little stupidly, fighting against her guilt, and the ridiculous desire to weep.

'I thought you said that you were not going with me tomorrow evening,' Theodore remarked when she had returned to her chair and was helping herself to a second cup of coffee.

'I changed my mind,' she explained, wincing as she filled the cup too much in her agitation and scalded her exploratory finger. 'Do you mind?'

'I'm thrilled, but——' He paused, plunging the living-room into a silence which was broken only by the ticking of the clock above the mantelshelf, then the newspaper crackled loudly in his hands. 'Roxy, don't play cat-and-mouse with Marcus.'

Roxy helped herself to milk and sugar, and sipped carefully at her coffee in an effort to gain time in which to control her voice, then she said with forced casualness, 'Daddy, I don't intend that we should meet again, if I can help it.'

'But why?' Theodore demanded incredulously, the newspaper crackling fiercely as if it was being man-handled before it landed on the floor beside his chair with a thud. 'I thought you were fond of him.'

'I *am* fond of him. Perhaps *too* fond of him,' she added with care. 'That's why I think it's time our friendship came to an end.'

There was a long perturbed silence, then Theodore sighed, 'I'm afraid I don't understand you.'

She smiled a little whimsically then. 'I don't think I understand myself, but there it is.'

Her father did not question her further, and merely picked up his newspaper and slapped it back on to his lap while she drank her coffee in silence before retiring to her workroom to catch up on the transcription she had neglected so much lately.

The evening spent at the home of their friends the Duncans left Roxy feeling bored and restless, and the evening out at Basil's golf club was not a success either. Her thoughts were taken up with Marcus to the extent that she felt like rushing to the nearest telephone just for the sake of hearing his voice.

Roxy ploughed through the evening somehow, smiling and laughing when it was expected of her, but craving inwardly to be near the one man who could make her feel so vitally alive. 'Oh, lord,' she thought at one time. 'Why couldn't I just be satisfied with the crumbs he had to offer me? The crumbs were so much better than this dead-weight emptiness inside of me.'

The party ended well after midnight, and she felt exhausted when Basil took her home. He had been unusually quiet that evening, but she had not attributed it to anything special until they arrived at her home.

He unlocked the door for her, and when he placed the key in her hand, he stopped her from going inside by placing his hands on her shoulders. 'We've known each other for a long time, Roxy,' he said, 'and you must know how I feel about you.'

If the concrete tiles had suddenly caved in beneath her she could not have been more surprised. 'Basil, please don't . . .'

'I love you, Roxy, and I want you to marry me,' he forestalled her urgently.

Of all things, she had never expected this, and never from Basil Vaughn. He was a man in his forties, not that his age mattered, but he had been her doctor since she was twelve, and later he had become her friend and employer. He had never once given any indication that he felt this way about her, and neither had she ever considered him as a would-be husband and lover. She could not for the life of her imagine why he should mention it now, and although she found the idea preposterous, she was nevertheless deeply touched.

'I'm afraid I—I can't marry you, Basil,' she said at last when she had found her voice.

His hands tightened their hold on her shoulders. 'Promise me you will at least think it over?'

'I promise, but——' She floundered, not wanting to hurt him, but knowing in her heart that she must speak the truth. 'Don't hope too much, Basil. I'm fond of you, but I—I don't love you.' She had never felt quite so dreadful in all her life, she thought as she added lamely, 'I'm sorry.'

'All I'm asking at the moment is that you think it over,' Basil persisted, brushing his lips against her cheek in a way he had done so often before. 'Goodnight, my dear.'

Roxy could not sleep that night. Basil's declaration had come as a shock to her, and she lay for hours going over everything in her mind. There had been no display of passion, no embarrassing overtures, just the calm statement that he loved her and wanted to marry her. She was thankful for his display of reticence, for it would at least make it easier for her when they met again, but it disturbed her to know that he felt that way about her. If he had mentioned his feelings a month ago, she might still have stopped to consider his proposal, but not now; not after knowing Marcus Fleming.

She should feel elated, she supposed. She had received her first proposal when she had thought never to receive any at all, but the incident had merely depressed her, and it had left her wondering why fate had so cruelly brought a man like Marcus into her life.

When morning came at last Roxy had not slept, and she climbed wearily out of bed to ring for Maggie before she went through to the bathroom to run her bath water.

'You're up early this morning, Miss Roxy,' Maggie remarked with disgusting cheerfulness when she walked into Roxy's bedroom five minutes later.

'I didn't sleep at all,' Roxy grumbled. 'What kind of day is it?'

'It's cold, Miss Roxy, and the lawns are white with frost,' Maggie told her. 'You'll have to wear something warm.'

'Slacks and a warm sweater will do,' Roxy decided listlessly, and leaving Maggie to select her clothes for her, she went through to the bathroom to soak away the fatigue of the hours she had tossed away in her bed that night.

'You look as though you never slept a wink,' Theodore remarked astutely when she joined him for breakfast an hour later. 'Did the evening out with Basil not live up to expectations?'

'As a matter of fact, my expectations were totally surpassed,' she replied tiredly as she seated herself at the table. 'He asked me to marry him.'

'He did *what*?' Theodore exploded, his knife and fork clattering on to his plate. 'I hope you didn't accept.'

'Oh, Daddy, how can you say that?' she frowned, regretting her impulse to tell her father about the incident. 'Basil is a wonderful man, and a fine doctor, and——'

'You don't love him,' Theodore cut in brusquely.

'No, I don't,' she admitted ruefully. 'But I did promise to consider his proposal.'

'I don't know how you could even think of giving him such a promise,' her father remonstrated agitatedly. 'The man must be out of his mind, and besides that, he's close on forty-five.'

'Daddy, if I loved him his age wouldn't matter at all, but I don't feel anything for him but fondness.'

'I should hope not!' Theodore snorted.

'Don't be unkind,' she protested.

'I'm sorry, Roxy,' he sighed. 'Now if it were Marcus——'

'It will *never* be Marcus,' she exclaimed heatedly, unconsciously twisting her table napkin up into a tight ball between her fingers. '*Never!*'

'My dear, I was merely supposing,' her father explained pacifyingly.

'Well, don't!' she snapped. There was a long, awkward silence, then she sighed and smiled waveringly. 'I'm sorry, Daddy. I'm bitchy this morning, and you really don't deserve that I should take it out on you.'

'What are fathers for, then?' Theodore laughed, and the tension eased at once as he got up and walked round to her side of the table to drop a light kiss on her forehead. 'See you this evening.'

Roxy sat there for some time, toying with a piece of toast, and finally settling for a cup of coffee. She had not expected her father to react so violently to the news that Basil had proposed to her, and she should, perhaps, have set his mind at ease, but when she considered how much Basil had done for her in the past she had felt obliged to defend him.

Oh, why was her life suddenly in such a mess? she wondered as she got up from the table and took a walk in the garden with Sheba at her side.

It was cold out, but she scarcely noticed. Her mind kept churning up incidents she would have preferred to forget, and she tortured herself with the memory of those blissful moments she had spent with Marcus when nothing had mattered beyond the touch of his lips and hands. When the cold finally penetrated the thickness of her sweater, making her shiver, she went inside to closet herself in her workroom, and for almost two hours she worked steadily on her transcriptions. The work occupied her mind, and she had almost succeeded in shutting out her painful thoughts when the door to her workroom was opened and closed firmly as if someone had entered.

No one, not even Maggie, would enter her workroom in that manner without announcing themselves in some way, and she stiffened, her head tilted in a listening attitude. She wished suddenly that she had brought Sheba in with her, for she would have given Roxy some idea of her unexpected caller's identity, but it was too late to wish that now.

'Who——?' she began nervously, but when those heavy footsteps approached her across the carpeted floor, she found herself experiencing those disturbing vibrations which she had encountered so often before, and she went hot and cold as she whispered hesitantly, 'Marcus?'

His particular brand of masculine cologne quivered in her nostrils, confirming her suspicions even before that deep, familiar voice murmured close to her ear, 'Clever guess, Roxy.'

CHAPTER FIVE

'CLEVER guess,' Marcus had said, but there had been no guessing involved in the discovery of his identity. No other man's presence had ever affected her in this alarming manner. They could be at opposite ends of a crowded room, and she would still know he was there, she thought.

'What are you doing here?' she asked nervously, then she heard him laugh that short, harsh laugh which always indicated his displeasure.

'Is that the way to welcome me after we've been away from each other for days?'

'Marcus, no!' she cried anxiously, leaping to her feet and moving a little out of his reach when she sensed instinctively that he was about to kiss her.

'What's the matter with you, Roxy?' he demanded tersely. 'You've been acting strangely ever since that night we went to Dave Whitby's housewarming party.'

'You're imagining things,' she lied desperately.

'Am I?' he remarked cynically. 'What happened that night?' he continued to question her after a frightening little silence. 'Did someone say something to you that could have brought on this sudden change in you?'

'Yes, *you!*' she wanted to shout at him, but how could she do so without revealing her feelings in the process, so she resorted to the lies she hated so much. 'No one said anything, and I haven't changed.'

She felt his eyes on her and knew that her cheeks were flushed. 'Have lunch with me today to prove it.'

'I can't,' she said stiffly. 'I'm going to the clinic in an hour's time, and I don't suppose I'll be finished there before late this afternoon.'

'And that's too late for me,' he told her harshly. 'I'm flying to Cape Town this afternoon, and I don't expect to get back until after the weekend.'

'That settles it, then,' she said dully.

'Does it?' She could almost feel the cynicism exuding from him, then something, presumably his fist, crashed down on to her desk, making her jump with fright. 'Damn you, Roxy! What's the matter with you?' he shouted at her. 'You've blown hot and cold on me, and I demand to know why!'

'If you want to know, then I'll tell you,' she shouted back at him, resorting to anger in her moment of stress. 'I think it's time our—our relationship ended, and I stand by what I told you initially. I don't want to become involved.'

'So it's that old worn-out story again about not wanting to be a burden because of your blindness, is it?' he demanded with hateful mockery. 'Well, I don't accept that, Roxy, and I'm damned if I'll let you get away with it.'

What did he mean? she wondered confusedly as she heard him move a few paces away from her, then the sound of a key being turned in the lock struck a chill of fear in her heart.

'Marcus?' she questioned hoarsely, and then, sensing the approach of danger like a trapped animal, she backed away, stumbling over the low coffee-table in her haste. She lost her balance and fell forward, but strong arms caught her before she reached the floor. She clutched wildly at the wide shoulders beneath the rough material of his jacket, but struggled for release against those restraining arms when she felt herself being lowered on to the leather sofa against the wall. 'Marcus, don't . . . I beg of you!'

Her pleas were ineffectual, and so were her struggles, for his hard body was relentless as he crushed her softness into the sofa. His breath was warm against her lips, and she turned her face away from that descending mouth, but he grasped a handful of her hair, sending a sharp pain through her scalp as he forced her face back to his, then that ruthless mouth was forcing hers into submission. She knew that she had to resist this onslaught, but she could not fight against the strength of those powerful arms, and much less could she fight against the emotions that swept through her like a tornado when she felt those warm, caressing hands against her skin beneath her sweater. She groaned inwardly, her lips moving of their own volition in passionate surrender beneath his as she admitted defeat, and a shudder of desire shook through her when the catch of her bra gave way beneath his fingers, giving him access to the fullness of her small, pointed breasts.

His hot, sensual mouth raked the sensitive cord of her throat while those caressing, probing fingers drew a moan of ecstasy from her soft, swollen lips. There was a delicious fire in her veins which drove all power of thought from her mind until she was conscious only of their hearts thudding in unison, and the aching need within her that lifted her beyond the realms of sanity.

'So you don't want to become involved, do you?' his taunting voice penetrated her drugged mind. 'Tell me how you're going to accomplish that feat when you've already involved yourself so deeply?'

Shame was like a shower of iced water preceding the fire of humiliation when he moved away from her, giving her the opportunity to restore a certain order of decency to her clothes. If she had proved anything, then she had proved just how easily he could arouse her emotions, she thought, and God help her if he should ever discover that she loved him.

'I won't be trifled with like a plaything you can discard when it pleases you,' she said in a voice that sounded raw to her own ears while she pushed her hair away from her white face with a trembling hand. 'I may be blind, but I do have feelings, and right this minute I despise you, Marcus Fleming!'

A long, angry silence followed her statement, then he asked roughly, 'Do you know what you're saying?'

'Yes,' she replied in a voice choked with anger. 'Go away, and leave me alone.'

She felt him hesitate, but she remained stubbornly silent, and a few moments later she heard the key crunch in the lock before the door was opened and closed quietly. She heard his footsteps growing faint down the passage, and minutes later the sound of a car being driven at speed down the drive reached her ears, then she slumped back on to the sofa and allowed the hot tears to slide from her lashes on to her cheeks.

Roxy realised only too well that she had brought to an end a brief but beautiful chapter in her life. It was best this way while she still had the courage to do what she knew she had to. There was no place for her in Marcus Fleming's life, and it had been foolish of her to imagine there might be. The solid black wall of her blindness was there between them and, added to that, his own admission that he preferred variety in women.

She felt desperately tired when she went upstairs to sponge her face and brush her hair before asking

Maggie to drive her to the clinic. The future was like an empty chasm before her that had to be filled somehow, and she would fill it in the only way she knew how.

It was fortunate, perhaps, that Roxy was kept busy at home and at the clinic during the days that followed. It gave her little time to brood over what had happened, and even less time to consider her own feelings in the matter. In time, she hoped, it would become nothing but a vague memory, but then, on the Tuesday morning of the following week, something occurred to bring the entire episode sharply into focus once more. Half way through the morning Maggie walked into Roxy's workroom and announced that a letter had arrived which was addressed to Roxy personally.

'A letter?' Roxy frowned curiously. 'But our post is never delivered at the house?'

'It was brought by special messenger,' Maggie told her. 'Do you want me to read it to you?'

Roxy leaned back in her chair and nodded. 'Yes, please.'

Maggie tore open the envelope, and there was the crackle of paper as she removed the letter from the envelope, then she said hesitantly, 'It's from Mr Fleming, Miss Roxy.'

Marcus! The thought of him brought forth a fresh stab of pain. What could he have to say to her that warranted a letter to be sent to her by special messenger?

'I don't imagine there'll be anything personal in it,' Roxy announced nervously, clenching her hands in her lap. 'Read it to me, Maggie.'

Maggie hesitated only briefly, then the paper crackled as she folded it open once more. 'Roxy,' she read, 'I returned from Cape Town yesterday, but will be snowed under with work for the rest of this week. I'm booked on the early evening flight to Rio de Janeiro on Friday, and I expect to be away approximately three weeks. There are important matters you and I have to discuss before I leave. Meet me at Carlo's for lunch on Friday at one o'clock sharp. If you're not there, then I shall take it you meant what you said at our last unfortunate meeting, and I shall not trouble you again in future. Marcus.'

'Would you read it to me again, Maggie?' Roxy whispered, leaning forward in her chair with a curiously breathless feeling in her chest as if the air had suddenly been squeezed from her lungs.

Maggie read it through once more and, when she had finished, Roxy held out her hand for the letter, and thanked her unsteadily.

'Are you going to meet him for lunch, Miss Roxy?' Maggie questioned inquisitively.

'I don't know,' Roxy replied, fingering the letter almost as if it afforded her the physical contact with Marcus which she had subconsciously yearned for.

'But, Miss Roxy, you——'

'Hello there!' Vera's familiar greeting interrupted their conversation, and Roxy placed a quick, soothing hand on Sheba's bristling neck as those high heels clicked across the floor towards her desk. 'Mummy asked me to drop by and give you these two complimentary tickets for the charity concert she's arranged for next Friday week,' Vera explained.

'Please thank your mother for me, Vera,' Roxy replied, putting the letter from Marcus aside. 'Would you like a cup of tea?'

'No, thanks. I must be off,' she declined, but for some reason she lingered in the room as Maggie ex-

cused herself. 'How's the affair?' she asked unexpectedly.

'Affair?' Roxy questioned in bewilderment.

'You and Marcus, of course,' Vera explained airily.

Roxy drew a careful breath. 'We're not having an
affair, Vera.'

'Oh, go on!' Vera laughed sarcastically. 'Marcus
Fleming isn't the type of man to have platonic relationships with women.'

'I assure you, I'm not having an affair with Marcus,'
Roxy replied, finding it increasingly difficult to keep
her anger in check.

'You'd be a fool not to,' Vera announced in that
familiar, breezy fashion. There was an odd little
silence, almost as if she had been distracted by
something, then she laughed softly and sighed, 'Oh,
well, that's your business, isn't it.'

Roxy's lips tightened. 'Yes, it *is* my business.'

'All right, Miss High and Mighty, I get the mes-
sage,' Vera exclaimed haughtily. 'See you around.'

She swept out of the room, her high heels tapping
on the floor, and Sheba grunted and slumped down
beside Roxy's chair as if she, too, was relieved that the
woman, whose perfume still lingered in the air, had
left.

Roxy stretched out a hand to where she had left the
letter. Had she been careless enough to leave it unfolded? she wondered vaguely, but as she raised the
paper to her lips she could think of nothing but the
unexpected invitation she had received from Marcus.

Should she meet him, or should she stay away? Her
mind warned that it would merely be a postponement
of the inevitable, but her heart differed. Was it possible that she had misunderstood? That she did, after
all, mean something to him? Why else would he want

her to meet him if it were not important to him that there should be some sort of understanding between them before he left for Rio de Janeiro? Could she risk ignoring his invitation and perhaps losing the only happiness she might ever know? No, she could not risk staying away, her heart warned, overruling the doubtful voice of her mind. She *would* meet him for lunch, even if it was for the very last time.

A new hope swept through her, leaving her light-hearted and excited at the prospect of being with Marcus again. God knew she had longed for his nearness and his touch with a hungry yearning that could not be assuaged, and that breathless, faintly eager note was back in her voice when she had tea with Basil in his office that afternoon.

'I have two complimentary tickets for the charity concert Mrs Sinclair has organised for next Friday evening,' she told him.

'Is this an invitation?' he asked with a smile in his voice, and the corners of her own mouth lifted.

'Naturally.'

There was a momentary silence in the small office where the smell of antiseptics mingled with that of the late autumn roses just outside the window, then Basil asked quietly, 'Have you given my proposal some thought?'

Roxy's smile disappeared slowly. 'Yes and no.'

'What does that mean?' Basil laughed a little curiously.

'Yes, I have given it thought, and, no ... I can't marry you.' She placed her cup carefully on his desk and clasped her hands tightly in her lap. What she regretted most about his proposal was the fact that the situation between them would never be the same again. She had lost a friend; someone she could rely on not to complicate her life, and it was also with this thought in mind that she added softly, 'I'm sorry, Basil.'

'So am I,' he admitted with surprising amiability, coming round his desk to place a heavy hand on her shoulder. 'I won't give up hoping, though. If you ever change your mind, just let me know.'

Roxy felt decidedly uncomfortable, but she sighed inwardly with relief when he changed the subject, and discussed one of his patients as if nothing unusual had occurred. She knew that he would not mention marriage again unless she felt inclined to discuss it, and that was unlikely, she decided, if anything was to come of her meeting with Marcus at the end of that week.

She was in her bedroom on the Friday morning, preparing herself for her lunch appointment with Marcus, when Maggie came in and said a little breathlessly, 'Miss Roxy, here's another letter for you.'

'From Mr Fleming?' Roxy asked, an inexplicable tension gripping her insides.

'Yes, Miss Roxy,' Maggie replied. 'It's typed this time, and not in an envelope.'

'Read it to me.'

Maggie cleared her throat, and read: 'Roxy, I must cancel our lunch appointment. I'm leaving on an earlier flight, and will contact you on my return. Marcus.'

Disappointment surged through Roxy, leaving her deflated, and filling her with the terrifying premonition that they would never meet again. It was silly, of course. Had he not said in his note that he would contact her on his return?

She was conscious suddenly of Maggie waiting for her to say something and, holding out her hand for the note, she said simply, 'Thank you, Maggie.'

Alone in her room a few minutes later, Roxy sat stiffly erect on the stool in front of the dressing table and, without consciously being aware of it, she tore the note into tiny fragments between her fingers. After the eagerness with which she had looked forward to this meeting, the anticlimax was almost too much to bear, and she choked back her tears with an angry exclamation on her lips. There was nothing for her to do now except to wait patiently for his return.

The three weeks passed with painful slowness from autumn into winter. Roxy heard from reliable sources that Marcus had returned from his trip to South America, but a further two weeks passed, and still he made no effort to contact her. It appeared that whatever he had wanted to discuss with her was no longer of any importance, and she decided dismally that, like so many other things in her life, she would have to resign herself to the knowledge that it had most probably all happened for the best.

This did not deter her pulses from fluttering wildly when she walked into her father's office one afternoon to find Marcus there, and it took some time for her to control herself sufficiently to speak.

'Marcus . . .' she began hesitantly, extending a nervous hand towards him.

His cold fingers touched hers briefly as he said abruptly, 'Good afternoon.'

Something was dreadfully wrong, she decided, sensing the animosity in him and, with the chill of winter in her heart, she tried again. 'Marcus, I wonder if——'

'Let me know as soon as you have this contract sorted out, will you, Theodore,' Marcus cut across her words rudely, and his manner sent the blood surging into her face.

'I'll do that, Marcus,' her father replied after an uncomfortable pause.

'Then you must excuse me. I have another appointment in a few minutes' time.'

Without a further word Marcus strode from the office, but the force of his presence lingered to taunt her confused and aching heart.

'What's happened between you two?' Theodore finally broke the strained, embarrassed silence, and Roxy emerged from her dazed, bewildered state with the humiliating suspicion that she had been thoroughly snubbed.

'I suppose you could say we had a difference of opinion,' she explained vaguely, trying to shrug off the after-effects of her unexpected meeting with Marcus. 'We were going to talk it over, but he had to fly to Rio de Janeiro at the time, and we just haven't had the opportunity to discuss it since his return.'

'He's been back two weeks.'

'I know.'

'Do you also know that he's seriously considering stationing himself in South America?'

Roxy felt as though her father had slammed his fist into her midriff. 'No, I didn't know.'

'If he does decide to go, then I understand it will be at the end of July. That's a little more than a month from now.'

'I see . . .' She swallowed convulsively. Would she ever learn to live with this hopeless pain tearing away at her insides? she wondered, then she buttoned up her coat with trembling fingers, almost as if she hoped it would help to keep out the hurt. 'Let's go home, Daddy.'

Roxy never knew afterwards how she managed to live through the next few days. She was conscious only of the despairing knowledge that time was running out on her, and that soon, within a few short weeks, the vast Atlantic Ocean would separate Marcus from her.

Her pace quickened with her disquieting thoughts as she walked down Eloff Street with her parcels in one hand while the other held on to Sheba's harness. At the corner of Jeppe Street, less than a block away from where Maggie was waiting with the car, Roxy ignored Sheba's urgent signals and stepped off the pavement. The squeal of brakes brought her to her senses, but at that moment she thought only of the faithful animal at her side. With an almost super-human effort she thrust Sheba back, but something hard slammed into her hip a second later, and she was sent spinning to the ground. There was a flash of pain shooting through her head, a scream that could only have come from her own lips, and then she mercifully knew no more.

Voices came and went, murmuring unintelligible phrases, and cool hands administered to her from time to time, but nothing registered until her father's anxious voice penetrated the thick layer of fog which had encased her mind.

'Roxy?' His familiar hand gripped hers tightly. 'How do you feel now?'

'I—I have a terrible headache,' she complained weakly, confused by the realisation that she was lying on a bed, and perturbed by the excruciating pain in her head when she tried to raise it. 'What—what happened?'

'You were knocked down by a car on the corner of Jeppe and Eloff Street.'

'Oh, yes . . . I remember now.' The memory of those squealing brakes flashed through her brain like a nightmare, and then a more pressing thought came to mind, making her clutch urgently at her father's hand as fear consumed her. 'Sheba?' she questioned, her voice rising sharply. 'What happened to Sheba?'

'She's at home, and there's absolutely nothing the matter with her,' he set her mind at rest quickly. 'You apparently pushed her back on to the pavement moments before that car struck you.'

'Thank heaven,' she croaked, unable to check the tears that filled her eyes, and it was some time before she spoke again. 'Daddy, will you telephone Basil and let him know I shan't be able to make it to the clinic this afternoon?'

There was an awkward silence, then her father said cautiously, 'Roxy, my dear . . . it's morning.'

'Morning?' Her mind groped wildly for understanding, but it evaded her.

'You've been unconscious since yesterday afternoon,' Theodore explained in a voice that was somehow shaky.

'Oh, lord!' she moaned. 'Was it as bad as that?'

'You were extremely fortunate,' Theodore explained with relief. 'You gashed the side of your head badly when you fell, but you have no other injuries except for a few nasty bruises.'

She fingered the starched sheets, and listened carefully to the hum of activity about her before she asked warily, 'Am I in hospital?'

'Yes,' Theodore admitted, moments before a nurse entered the ward to announce that it was time for him to leave. He stood up at once and leaned over Roxy to kiss her on the cheek. 'I'll see you again this evening,' he whispered, and then she found herself alone with a silent but efficient nurse who took her pulse and her temperature before checking the dressing high up against her hairline where her head still continued to throb painfully.

Roxy was allowed home a few days later when the stitches had been removed, and when the doctor had satisfied himself that she was well enough to leave the hospital, but the incessant headaches she suffered during the following week finally drove her into Basil Vaughn's consulting-rooms.

He examined her carefully, and she knew the ritual only too well to realise that he was flashing lights into her eyes. It filled her with a vague feeling of discomfort on this occasion, and she was relieved when he finally arranged for her to be X-rayed.

'What's wrong with me, Basil?' she wanted to know when she emerged from the X-ray department to find him waiting for her.

'Can't tell yet,' he said abruptly. 'That's why I wanted you X-rayed.'

'Have you no idea at all?'

There was a strained silence, then he took her arm and escorted her out to her car. 'I have an idea what it might be, but I'd rather not discuss it until I'm certain of my facts.'

'You're beginning to frighten me.'

'You have nothing to be afraid of. Oh, and here——' He thrust a packet into her hands as Maggie approached to take charge of her. 'Take two of these capsules for the headache, but there must be six hours between each dosage. They're pretty powerful.'

Three days later Roxy and her father were summoned to Basil's consulting-rooms, and the mere fact that her father had been asked to accompany her made Roxy realise that, whatever Basil had to tell them, it was something extremely serious. It filled her with trepidation and fear, and she broke out in a cold sweat when they were finally ushered into his office.

'I'm glad you could come, Mr Cunningham,' Basil

said, his voice professionally frightening as he assisted Roxy into a chair. 'I have the X-rays set up for you to examine them.'

Theodore accompanied Basil to the other side of the room and the sound of a switch being flicked jarred against Roxy's nerves.

'But these are the X-rays you took some years ago,' Theodore protested at once.

'I'm well aware of that,' Basil replied calmly. 'I'd like you to take a close look at them before I illustrate the result of Roxy's accident two weeks ago, so bear with me, please.'

There was a tense, lingering silence, then Roxy said impatiently, 'Don't keep us in suspense, Basil.'

'Very well,' he laughed briefly, but she knew him too well not to detect the underlying note of strain in his laughter. 'You see here the tiny steel fragment, and it's no bigger than the tip of a lead pencil,' he proceeded to enlighten her father. 'It entered through her temple, severed a large vein, and miraculously travelled behind her eyes without injuring them, but then it severed the optic chiasma and settled in the spongy bone beyond it.' Roxy's clever ears picked up the sound of X-ray plates being removed and replaced with others. 'Now I'd like you to look at the X-rays taken a few days ago,' Basil was saying. 'The blow she received on her head when she fell has altered the position of the bone fragments and the fragment of grenade. It appears now that the optic nerves had only been partially severed, and that the loss of function had been caused by the pressure of the bone fragments and metal on the nerves.'

There was a long, strained silence during which it seemed that even the furniture was holding its breath, then Theodore asked the question that stood out glaringly in Roxy's mind.

'What does this mean?'

'Now that the pressure has been lifted slightly, it appears that the optic nerves are still sending impulses through to the brain. Look, I'll demonstrate this.' He crossed the room to Roxy's side and adjusted her position slightly, then he retreated once more and said abruptly, 'Hold that position, Roxy.' He flicked a switch, and she experienced again that vague feeling of discomfort before he spoke to Theodore. 'Do you see how her pupils are reacting to the light?'

'Yes, I see,' her father acknowledged this discovery.

Another flick of the switch removed her discomfort, and as a long, drawn-out silence threatened once more, she said irritably, 'Cut out the dramatics, Basil, and tell us the bare facts. Is there a possibility now that you can operate, or isn't there?'

Basil cleared his throat uncomfortably. 'Yes . . . and no.'

'Explain yourself,' she ordered sharply, her hands clenched so tightly in her lap that her fingers ached.

'There's a possibility that I could operate now that the pressure has been lifted and the optic nerves appear not to have been severed entirely, but——'

'But?' she prompted impatiently. 'Come on, Basil! I've lived long enough with the knowledge that I'll always be blind, so let's have it straight, and I can promise you there won't be any hysterics.'

'It's a dangerous operation,' Basil told them now without further hesitation. 'That tiny piece of steel and the fragments of bone have eased the pressure on the nerves, but they've moved dangerously close to the brain. If I operate there's a strong possibility that you'll regain your sight partially . . . even entirely, but it could also result in severe brain damage.'

Roxy could not have explained her feelings at that moment even if she had tried. She had lived so long without hope that it made little difference to her at that moment whether her sight was restored to her or not. But as the seconds ticked by she began to think differently, although a built-in wariness made her reject that tiny flicker of hope even before it had taken shape.

'What are the chances?' her father asked at last.

'Fifty-fifty,' Basil replied with blunt sincerity. 'It's a risk whichever way you look at it.'

'What do you suggest?' asked Roxy, finding her voice at last.

'I wouldn't advise the operation—not yet, anyway,' Basil told her quite firmly. 'I'd like to study the X-rays further, and consult a few of my colleagues here in South Africa and abroad. When I've been informed of their opinions, I'll let you know, but in the meantime don't build up your hopes too much.'

Roxy and her father drove home in abject silence, each occupied with their own frightening thoughts, but when they were in the house Theodore drew Roxy into his arms, and held her tightly.

'I'd give every cent I possess for your sight to be restored to you,' he said thickly, 'but if there's the slightest risk involved, then you must forgive me if I withhold my consent.'

Roxy said nothing, but she tightened her arms about him in despair. She knew his fears as if they were her own, and she knew, too, the futility of hoping too much. The first five years of her blindness had been spent praying for miracles, but she had eventually been forced to resign herself to the fact that she would remain blind for the rest of her life. Now, after all these years, fate had decided to present her with the suggestion of a miracle, but it felt as though she had been given a scorpion with a deadly sting in its tail.

CHAPTER SIX

THE possibility of having an operation some day in the future was never discussed between Roxy and her father, but it was there; the unmentionable yet ever-present subject that lurked like a stealthy shadow in their minds, and thrusting long, strained silences between them.

'I met an old acquaintance of mine today,' Theodore told her after dinner one evening when one of those awkward silences threatened between them. 'It's Jim McGregor. You may not remember him, but I once did a lot of work for his company in Zimbabwe, and I understand now that he's been living here in Johannesburg for the past year.'

'Jim McGregor?' Roxy frowned momentarily, then her brow cleared. 'I seem to remember that his daughter Constance was in my class at school.'

'That's correct, yes. She's married now and living in Australia.'

Constance McGregor had been blonde, fragile-looking, and an ingrate snob who had made herself unpopular with most of the children in the class, Roxy recalled vividly, and although her interest waned instantly, she said politely, 'You must have had a lot to talk about after all these years.'

'We did, yes,' Theodore admitted enthusiastically. 'We had lunch together, and he told me, incidentally, that it was Marcus who'd told him how to contact me.'

'Marcus?' she questioned with quickening interest while trying to ignore the stab of pain at the mention of his name.

'They met on a flight to Rio de Janeiro last month,' her father explained. 'They actually met before their flight left that evening while they were having a drink in the lounge, and——'

'Evening?' she interrupted sharply, every nerve vibratingly alive and alert as she clutched at the arms of her chair and repeated urgently, 'Did you say evening?'

'As far as I know there's only that one flight to Rio de Janeiro on a Friday evening, but why do you ask?'

'Oh, God!' she groaned, her mind in a state of confusion at the surprising discovery she had made.

What did it mean? What *could* it mean? Was it possible that somewhere, somehow, something had gone wrong? A misunderstanding, perhaps? Why send her a note saying that he would be leaving on an earlier flight when there *was* no earlier flight? And why neglect to contact her as he had stated in the note, and then treat her in that offhanded manner as if she were the guilty party? It just did not make sense! She had not delved into the subject so deeply before, but, now that she stopped to consider, it seemed so unlike Marcus to behave in that manner.

'Roxy, what is it?' her father interrupted her puzzled thoughts, and without hesitation, she confided in him.

'I had an appointment to have lunch with Marcus that day he left for Rio de Janeiro. It was rather important, but then I received a note from him that Friday morning telling me he couldn't meet me as arranged because he was leaving on an earlier flight.' She bit her lip to control its trembling. 'Do you suppose he changed his mind about meeting me, and then took the easy way out by lying about his departure time?'

'That doesn't sound like Marcus,' her father said at once. 'If he'd changed his mind about meeting you, then he would have come right out and told you so instead of misleading you with lies.'

'That's what I thought,' she murmured distractedly, her mind running riot. Was it possible that he had waited for her that day at Carlo's? But why send that note cancelling their appointment? The more she thought about it, the more bewildered and confused she became, but one thing was certain – she was going to find out exactly what happened and, jumping up to ring through for Maggie, she said: 'Daddy, I must go out. It's important.'

'You can't go out alone at this time of night,' her father protested instantly, following her across the room.

'Daddy, I *must*!' she cried desperately, and at the sound of footsteps approaching the hall, she turned and said quickly, 'Maggie, get the car out while I fetch my coat.'

'Where do you want to go to at this time of night, Miss Roxy?' Maggie demanded in astonishment.

'I'll explain on the way.'

Her father's hand came down on her arm. 'You may go on condition that you take Sheba with you, but I hope you know what you're doing, Roxy.'

'I hope so too,' she admitted, placing her hand over his and squeezing it lightly. 'Oh, I hope so too!'

She felt excited and afraid simultaneously as Maggie drove her into the city with a panting Sheba seated in the back of the car. She was acting intuitively, and it could lead to nothing, but it was worth a try. She might end up making a fool of herself once again, but she would not rest until she had solved this puzzling mystery. There might, of course, be no mystery attached to the incident at all, she told herself, chewing her bottom lip nervously, but she had to make sure of that.

Carlo was having a busy night, judging from the sound of activity that reached Roxy's ears when Maggie left her at the entrance to the restaurant, but he came to her at once and raised her hand to his lips in his usual latin manner.

'Signorina Cunningham,' he said with genuine warmth. 'This is an honour.'

'Carlo, I need some information.'

'And a cup of good strong Italian coffee,' he insisted, drawing her towards a quiet table and seating himself opposite her. The coffee arrived a few seconds later as if it had been there waiting for her, and only when she had swallowed down almost half the contents of her cup did he ask, 'What kind of information did you want, *signorina*?'

Now that the moment had come, Roxy felt foolishly nervous, and she clenched her hands tightly in her lap to stop them from shaking. 'Do you recall whether Marcus came to lunch here one Friday afternoon last month? On the twelfth, to be exact?'

'That is a difficult question, *signorina*,' Carlo replied. 'He has lunch here sometimes, but I cannot say for certain that he was here on the day you mentioned.'

'On the Friday I'm referring to he may have been waiting for someone to join him,' Roxy tried again. 'Does that help at all?'

'*Si, si*, I think so,' Carlo told her after a moment of careful deliberation. 'He came in here and sat down at his usual table, but he did not order lunch. *Si*, that is right. He was waiting for someone, he said, and he waited for almost an hour, but when this person did not arrive . . . he left.'

She sucked her breath in sharply and felt a little sick as she visualised Marcus waiting there for her while she had sat at home nursing her disappointment after receiving that note telling her he had to cancel their meeting.

'Did he—did he look upset?' she asked hesitantly.

'He looked *very* angry, *signorina*,' Carlo told her with strong emphasis. 'Do you know who he was waiting for that day?'

'Yes,' she nodded miserably. 'He was waiting for me.'

'Ah!' he muttered sympathetically. 'You had been having a lovers' argument?'

'Not exactly,' she smiled with faint amusement, 'but it was very important at the time that we should meet and talk things over, and—and I had every intention of coming, but then I—I received that note.'

'A note, *signorina*?'

'A note telling me that he couldn't make it,' she explained.

'But why should he send a note to say that he could not meet you when he was here waiting for you all the time?' Carlo demanded in confused astonishment.

Roxy sighed heavily. 'That's something I wish I understood myself, Carlo.'

'Perhaps someone was making a joke,' he proffered hesitantly.

'A joke?' She bit her lip and frowned. 'Who would want to play a cruel joke like that? And who would have known we were to meet each other here and then set about doing such a terrible thing?'

'A woman, perhaps,' Carlo suggested at length. 'A jealous woman can do terrible things, *signorina*.'

'Yes, but *who*?'

Even as she asked the question a curtain of fog

seemed to lift from her mind. She recalled that morning in detail when she had received that first letter from Marcus asking her to meet him for lunch on the Friday. Maggie had read the letter to her before placing it in her hand, and then Vera had walked in with those tickets for the charity concert. Roxy recalled placing the folded letter on her desk, but, when Vera had left, the letter had lain there unfolded. Yes, she remembered now thinking it strange at the time, but her thoughts had been so taken up with Marcus that the incident had made no impression on her at all.

'You have thought of someone?' Carlo interrupted her thoughts curiously.

'Yes, but——' She paused guiltily. 'Oh, I don't know. She couldn't have—she wouldn't have, surely, but——'

'It is possible, *si*?' Carlo prompted.

'Yes, it's possible,' she was forced to admit, albeit reluctantly. Vera had sounded more than ordinarily bitchy that morning, and no one else but she could have thought up such a clever way of causing trouble, Roxy realised in dismay as she rose to her feet and held out her hand to the man opposite her. 'Carlo . . . thank you so much. You've helped me tremendously.'

'I am always at your service, *signorina*,' he said with a warm smile in his voice as he raised her hand to his lips, then her escorted her to where Maggie was waiting for her in the car. '*Arrivederci, signorina.*'

'*Arrivederci*, Carlo,' she smiled, and then Maggie was swerving the car into the traffic.

'Did you find out anything, Miss Roxy?' Maggie wanted to know.

'Yes, I did,' she replied abruptly, evading Sheba's cold nose in her neck. 'I'm almost certain now that the note never came from Mr Fleming.'

'What do you mean, Miss Roxy?'

'Never mind,' she said impatiently. 'You have the address, so take me to Mr Fleming's flat.'

'But, Miss Roxy, you can't go to a man's flat at this time of night,' Maggie exclaimed in dismay. 'It wouldn't look right.'

'I don't particularly care what it looks like, Maggie,' she retorted anxiously. 'It's very important to me that this misunderstanding be cleared between Mr Fleming and myself, and to do that I must speak to him. I *must* explain.'

'But, Miss Roxy——'

'Please, Maggie,' she interrupted tiredly as she felt her headache returning. 'Don't argue. Just take me there.'

Maggie muttered something under her breath, but she knew that once Roxy had made up her mind about something, nothing would dissuade her, so she drove on to the address Roxy had once asked her to look up out of curiosity.

The building they entered some minutes later was expensive-looking and still comparatively new, Maggie informed Roxy as they crossed the foyer to where the names of the tenants were listed, but Roxy had little interest in anything at that moment except the reason for her presence there.

'Which floor?' she demanded abruptly, her hand tightening on Sheba's harness.

'The sixth, Miss Roxy,' Maggie answered. 'Number 603.'

'Come on,' Roxy said impatiently, and when they stood in the lift carrying them up to the sixth floor, she asked, 'Which is the ground floor button?'

'Bottom left,' Maggie replied, and Roxy's fingers explored the control buttons to familiarise herself with them.

The lift came to a smooth halt and the doors slid open with a minimum of noise, but when they stepped out of it Roxy paused and said nervously, 'Describe the place to me, please.'

'There are three flats on this floor, Miss Roxy. One to the left of where you are standing, one straight ahead, and one to the right.'

'Which is Mr Fleming's?'

'The one to your right,' said Maggie with obvious reluctance. 'It's about ten steps from here, Miss Roxy, and the doorbell is on the right side of the door.'

'Thank you.'

'Shall I wait for you, Miss Roxy?'

'Downstairs in the foyer, yes, and take Sheba with you to keep you company.'

'Miss Roxy . . .'

'Stop worrying,' Roxy smiled nervously, placing Sheba in Maggie's care. 'Just go and wait downstairs. I'll manage perfectly well on my own.'

Maggie mumbled something unintelligible, but the lift doors opened and closed, and then Roxy was alone. Ten steps, Maggie had said, and pacing them off Roxy found herself almost directly in front of a panelled door. Her hand found a small button to the right of the door, but at that point her courage seemed to desert her. Her nerves had become knotted at the pit of her stomach, and her heart was beating so hard and fast in her breast that she felt ridiculously faint. She doubted suddenly whether it had been wise of her to come to Marcus's flat in this manner. How would he receive her? And what if he no longer cared? Her finger hovered over the button, trembling with indecision, but then she knew she had to make the effort to clear up the misunderstanding which had created such an insurmountable barrier between them. A bell chimed somewhere behind that panelled door and, after what seemed like an eternity, the door was opened.

'Roxy!' That deep, well-modulated voice registered a measure of surprise, but it was cold to the point of rudeness when he demanded harshly, 'What are you doing here at this time of night, and what do you want?'

There was a smothered feeling in her chest, and a dryness in her throat as she found herself stammering, 'I—I'd like to talk to you, if I may.'

'I can't think of anything we have to say to each other.'

'Marcus, please,' she begged hoarsely, running the tip of her tongue across her dry lips. 'It's important.'

'Then say what you have to say, and go back to where you came from.'

It was like a slap in the face, and she felt that humiliating warmth surge into her cheeks as she said unsteadily, 'It wasn't easy coming here this evening.'

'Congratulations,' he returned sarcastically.

'Please . . .' Somewhere inside Beethoven's Appassionata Sonata was playing softly, poignantly, and gathering the remnants of her courage, she pleaded softly, 'Let me explain, Marcus.'

'Explain about what?'

'That day I was supposed to meet you at Carlo's—' she began, but she broke off abruptly when she heard him utter a disparaging sound.

'There's nothing to explain that I don't already know,' he told her in that cold, unrelenting manner that seemed to stab her right through the heart. 'My letter to you was most explicit, and you acted upon it as you chose to at the time. I understood, and that's all there is to it.'

Roxy drew a shaky breath. 'But I didn't——'

'Who's at the door, Marcus?' a smooth, feminine voice cut across Roxy's denial, and it sent the blood flowing like ice through her veins.

'No one of importance, Gail,' Marcus delivered the final blow, and Roxy clutched at the door-frame for support when she felt herself swaying, then, through the veil of her misery, she heard that mocking voice enquire, 'You were saying, Roxy?'

It was several seconds before she could speak, and when she did her voice sounded odd, and distant to her own ears. 'It doesn't matter,' she said. 'I'm sorry. It was a mistake to come.'

She turned, knowing that his eyes followed her slow, uncertain steps in the general direction of the lift, but he offered her no assistance, and neither would she have accepted it. She fumbled for the button which would send the lift up to her, her back stiff and erect, but when those steel doors finally enclosed her in that small, confined cage, she sagged against the wall and shivered uncontrollably as a deathly coldness made its way along every nerve and sinew of her body.

What a *fool* she had been, she thought bitterly, and she laughed a little hysterically as the lift bore her down to the ground floor. What a fool! What an *idiot* to imagine that the incident had left him equally disturbed and unhappy. For Marcus it had become something of the past, while his present, and possibly his future, was up there in his flat with him, waiting impatiently for him to return to her arms the moment he had got rid of the nuisance at the door.

'Oh, God,' she thought, pressing her fingers against her temples. 'If only this pain would stop then maybe I'd be able to think straight.'

Maggie was in the foyer to meet Roxy when she stepped out of the lift, and Roxy's hand was taken at once and placed on Sheba's harness. They walked out of the building in silence, and it was not until Maggie had steered the car into the late evening traffic that she asked curiously,

'Did you speak to Mr Fleming, Miss Roxy?'

'I spoke to him.'

Maggie remained silent as if she expected Roxy to elaborate, then she asked with a measure of uncertainty in her voice, 'Is everything settled now?'

'Everything is settled,' Roxy replied dully, her head throbbing now as if a sledge-hammer was beating against her temples.

'I'm glad, Miss Roxy.'

'So am I, Maggie,' Roxy answered tiredly, leaning her head back against the seat. 'So am I.'

When they arrived at the house she went up to her room at once and swallowed down one of the capsules Basil had prescribed for her headache. She bathed and changed into a nighty and a warm bath robe, but she did not get into bed. Instead, she sat down on the padded window-seat and listened to the night sounds through her partially opened window. It was a cold night, but she seemed not to notice while her mind was occupied with the feverish thoughts that cascaded through it.

She had known from the start that she would be the one to suffer if she allowed herself to become involved with Marcus, but she had been drawn to him like a moth to a lighted candle. It was inevitable that her wings would become singed, and her pain was like a flame devouring her. What a gullible fool she had been; an innocent playing at a game which had required a woman of experience, and the rules had

firmly excluded the word 'love'. Dear heaven! She had
not wanted to love him, but it had crept up on her
stealthily and swiftly until she could no longer deny it
to herself. She had wanted to end their relationship,
but then his letter had arrived, and she had changed
her mind about never seeing him again. Now, as a
result of Vera's obvious interference, it was over, and
she knew that, deep down in her heart, she had never
wanted to end it at all. She loved Marcus too much,
and too deeply, but fate had determined differently,
and here she was, left out in the cold while someone
else continued the game and played it according to the
unspoken rules.

'Oh, Marcus, Marcus . . .' she whispered agonis-
ingly into the night, and all her pain and despair was
interned in the mention of his name.

Silent tears rolled down her cheeks and fell un-
heeded on to her hands where they lay limply in her
lap. She made no effort to restrain them, and they
continued to flow until she felt drained and devoid of
feeling.

Her tears had long since dried on her cheeks when
there was a light tap on her bedroom door, and
moments later her father's heavy footsteps crossed the
room towards her.

'Roxy?' he questioned quietly. 'Where did you go to
this evening?'

To lie to her father did not occur to her, and she
said quite clearly, 'I went to see Marcus after making a
few enquiries at Carlo's restaurant.'

There was a brief silence as if he were digesting her
statement, then he asked, 'Did you sort out the misunderstanding?'

'Yes,' she said, and in truth that was not a lie.

'Would you like to talk about it?' Theodore persisted, detecting something in her manner which obviously disturbed him.

'No,' she shook her head. 'There's nothing to talk about.'

'I'll leave you, then.'

'Daddy?' she began as he turned from her. 'Sit down a minute.'

He did as she requested and took the hands she extended towards him, his fingers tightening about hers and offering the comfort she needed. 'What is it, my dear?' he questioned her urgently.

'Daddy, I know this is going to be difficult for you, but——' She paused momentarily, searching for the right words. She knew what she wanted now, and all that remained for her to do was to convince her father. 'I want to take that chance Basil offered me. I don't want to wait. I want him to operate.'

'Roxy, no!' Theodore exclaimed in anguish, his hands shaking as they held hers.

'Please, Daddy. *Please!*' she begged feverishly. 'I've got to take that chance. Don't you see?'

'We'll talk about it tomorrow,' her father tried to dismiss the subject, but Roxy was equally determined to thrash it out that very minute.

'We'll talk about it *now*,' she insisted, a calm, deadly determination taking possession of her. 'I've made up my mind. It's all . . . or nothing.'

Preferably nothing, she thought secretly. There was nothing left to live for, only the memory of harsh words cutting her to the core.

'Do you know what you're asking of me, Roxy?' her father asked, defeat in every syllable he seemed to utter with such difficulty.

'I know what I'm asking,' she replied, her compassionate heart understanding what it would mean to him if the operation were a failure, but she also knew what it would mean to her. It would be a release from the pain and the despair of loving unwisely and, next to having her sight restored, that was what she wanted more than anything on earth at that moment. 'I know I'm most probably being selfish,' she said at length, 'but whatever happens, I can't go on like this.'

She was in his arms then, burying her face against the roughness of his dressing gown and inhaling the familiar scent of him. She felt suddenly incredibly tired, as if it had taken a tremendous effort to reach this decision to have the operation, and she leaned against him heavily, remembering how, during that first year of her blindness, she had fallen asleep in his arms many a night because she had feared those ominously silent hours after sunset.

Roxy awakened the following morning with the feeling that she had lived through a nightmare, but it did not alter her decision, and when Basil Vaughn walked into his consulting-rooms at ten-thirty that morning, she was waiting to speak to him.

'Come through, Roxy,' he said, taking her arm and ushering her into the other room. 'Sit down. There's a chair beside you.'

She lowered herself on to the chair and waited until she heard his own chair creak on the opposite side of the desk before she spoke. 'What have you heard from your colleagues?'

'Nothing constructive as yet.'

'How do you feel about it personally?'

'Still the same, I'm afraid,' he sighed. 'It's a risk I wouldn't advise at this point.'

'I want to take that risk, Basil.'

There was a startled, incredulous silence, then he

said laughingly, 'You're joking, of course.'

'On the contrary,' she told him quietly, 'I'm serious about it.'

'You must be out of your mind, Roxy!' he exclaimed anxiously. 'Do you know what could happen to you if the operation fails?'

'Yes,' she shrugged carelessly. 'I end up an imbecile who's better off dead.'

'Don't joke about it!' he snapped, the rollers of his chair squealing across the floor as he rose to his feet with obvious agitation.

'I'm not joking,' she assured him calmly. 'I'm asking you to perform the operation.'

'I refuse!' he almost shouted at her.

'And I insist!'

There was a mutinous silence, then Basil said tersely, 'You're forgetting something. I shall need your father's consent to do this operation, and he'll never give it.'

Roxy smiled faintly for the first time. 'My father has given his consent verbally, and he'll give it officially on paper when the time comes.'

'You must both be mad!' Basil exploded, coming round to her side of the desk to grasp her hands. 'Roxy, for God's sake, it's your life you're trifling with so carelessly.'

'Do it for me, Basil,' she insisted persuasively. 'If I'm willing to take the chance, then why can't you?'

'Can't you wait a little longer until——'

'No!' she interrupted with a sharp edge to her voice, then she controlled herself and added in a softer tone, 'I've reached the end, Basil. One way or another, it doesn't matter.'

'What's come over you? I've never known you like this,' he said at length, drawing her up out of her chair and shaking her a little as if he wanted to shake some sense into her. 'You've always taken my advice in the past, so why won't you take it now?'

'Will you perform the operation, Basil, or do I get someone else to do it?' she counter-questioned, clinging desperately to the patience she had always prided herself on possessing.

'Do you think I'd trust anyone else to lay a finger on you?' he demanded roughly, his hands tightening on her shoulders.

'Then you will do it?'

There was a long silence, fraught with conflicting thoughts, and she knew he was finding it difficult to agree to an operation he did not have total confidence in, just as her father had found it difficult giving his consent.

'I'll do it, if that's what you really want,' Basil sighed at last, but she could hear by the tone of his voice that he was not at all happy about it.

'How soon?'

'Next month?' he said hopefully, but she shook her head.

'This week,' she stated adamantly. 'Tomorrow, if possible.'

'My God!' His hands shook, and he released her abruptly. 'I'll make the necessary arrangements and let you know when to come into the clinic.'

He had sounded, all at once, over-professional, but Roxy, who knew him better, realised that it was the shield behind which he so successfully hid his personal feelings. She knew that he loved her, that he had asked her not so long ago to marry him, and she knew what it could do to him if she was reduced to a helpless object kept alive by machinery until God mercifully took what was left of her.

Was she being selfish? she wondered as she murmured 'Thank you,' and left his consulting-rooms. Was it selfishness to think only of herself and not of those who cared for her; those who would have to stand by helplessly, watching her waste away day by day if the operation failed to restore her sight, but succeeded in giving her what she craved most at that moment—a sort of limbo state before death?

Questions whirled through her mind while Maggie drove her home; questions for which she found no answers, but she had gone steadily beyond the stage of caring, and there was only one road ahead which she cared to take. God only knew where it would lead, but to her it did not matter.

Roxy was admitted to the clinic the following afternoon, and preparations began in earnest for the operation which Basil was to perform two days later. There were X-rays and tests, and long, intricate discussions with the surgeons who were to assist, and there was her father, hovering by her side and refusing to leave. Roxy did not have the heart to send him away, and he spent that last night beside her bed, holding her hand even when the sedative they had given her had taken effect.

CHAPTER SEVEN

A preliminary medication left Roxy drowsily content as they wheeled her smoothly along the passages from the ward to the theatre. She was not afraid; she was not even vaguely perturbed at the thought of what might happen, but when her father came up to her moments before they wheeled her into the operating theatre, she heard the anxiety in his voice, and felt it in his touch.

Basil was there as well, bending over her to speak into her ear. 'There's still time to change your mind, Roxy.'

'I'm not going to change my mind,' she answered drowsily but firmly. 'Whatever happens, I know you'll do your best.'

'Don't disfigure her too much,' she heard her father say. 'She's suffered enough over the years.'

'I shall be cutting above the hairline, Mr Cunningham,' Basil replied professionally. 'When her hair grows out again it will cover the scar completely.'

'How long will the operation last?'

'That's difficult to say. Three, maybe four hours,' Basil answered vaguely, not wanting to commit himself.

'Daddy?' Roxy tightened her fingers about her father's hand. 'Don't worry too much, and . . . thank you . . . for everything.'

She was wheeled into the theatre after that, and she was conscious of the activity about her as she was transferred from the trolley on to the operating table. The atmosphere seemed tense when the anaesthetist announced that he was ready. Basil murmured, 'Go ahead', and then Roxy knew no more until she found herself drifting in a world of bright, flashing colours.

Was she in heaven or was she in hell? she wondered crazily, then she heard a voice demanding repeatedly, 'Roxy, can you hear me?'

The voice was vaguely familiar, but she drifted away, deeper into this abyss of whirling stars and beyond to where the darkness offered blessèd relief.

Again and again that voice recalled her to consciousness until she was forced to recognise it as her father's.

'I hear you,' she managed at last with a measure of annoyance and irritation. 'Why didn't Basil operate?'

'Basil operated this morning, my dear,' her father told her with an odd inflection in his voice. 'You're going to be all right.'

'Oh, God,' she moaned, disappointment bringing her to full consciousness. 'Why?'

'Why? What do you mean, Roxy?'

'I wanted to die,' she croaked out her misery.

'You wanted to——'

'Take it easy, Mr Cunningham. Perhaps it would be a good idea if you left now, and I suggest you try to get some rest.'

Roxy recognised that voice at once, and turned her head in its direction to cry out in despair, 'Basil, why, why?'

'Relax, my dear,' he soothed her, his hands holding her down against the pillows. 'You need plenty of rest.'

There was a pin-prick in her arm, and then she drifted off into that mad world from which she had emerged minutes before, but on this occasion she drifted further and slept naturally.

She was fully conscious, however, the following morning when Basil came in to ask how she was feeling.

'I feel as though I'm going crazy,' she complained. 'I'm in a Technicolor madhouse and it's . . . it's quite indescribable.'

'That will ease off eventually,' he told her, holding on to her hand long after he had taken her pulse. 'What you're experiencing at the moment is caused by the nerves coming alive now that the pressure has been lifted completely.'

'Was the operation a success?'

'You're alive, aren't you?' he laughed teasingly, but there was no answering smile on her lips as she raised a tentative hand to her eyes.

There were no restricting bandages covering them, and yet there was only that Technicolor blankness. 'Why can't I see?'

'It's going to take time,' Basil warned her calmly. 'The nerves had been pinched for a long time, and the healing process will be gradual before they start functioning properly again.'

'How long?' she demanded abruptly.

'Two weeks—a month—perhaps longer.'

'Perhaps never,' she added cynically, her initial disappointment replaced by the urgent desire to be able to see.

'I'm confident that you *will* see, Roxy,' Basil told her firmly. 'Just be patient, and give it time.'

'Yes,' she sighed, a faint smile hovering about her mouth now. 'There's plenty of time.'

Before he left the ward Basil issued a few instructions to the nursing Sister in attendance, and a few minutes later Roxy drifted off into an easy sleep once more. She slept away most of the day, hovering between consciousness and oblivion until her father entered her ward that evening and approached her bed.

'Roxy?'

She opened her eyes and turned them blindly in his direction. 'Hello, Daddy.'

'How do you feel now?' he asked anxiously, and she heard a chair scraping on the floor before he took her hand in his.

'I feel as though I have a hole in the head,' she smiled faintly. 'How is everyone at home?'

'We all miss you very much. Most especially Sheba.'

'Poor Sheba,' she sighed tiredly. 'Take care of her for me, Daddy.'

'You know I will,' he promised.

'I'm sorry I upset you yesterday,' she said selfconsciously. 'Forgive me?'

'Of course I forgive you,' Theodore brushed aside her apology. 'It was merely the after-effects of the operation that made you feel that way.'

Roxy did not contradict him. There was no purpose in upsetting him once more with an explanation of the reasons for her ridiculous desire for death, and they talked quietly and a little awkwardly for a time, neither of them mentioning the serious side of the operation she had survived.

'Roxy, I'm going to leave you now,' her father said eventually, and she felt him lean towards her urgently. 'There's someone else waiting to see you, and he's been waiting very anxiously since yesterday morning to have a word with you.'

'Who is it?' she asked hesitantly, an odd tension gripping her.

'Marcus.'

'Marcus?' she repeated in anguish, then her control seemed to snap and, as if from some distance away, she heard herself crying out in a near-hysterical voice, 'No! Oh, no, no! Send him away! I don't want him here! Send him away!'

'Please wait outside, Mr Cunningham,' an authoritative voice instructed, and Roxy clutched wildly at the arms that held her down.

'Send him away, Basil. Don't let him in here. Please, I don't want——'

'Sister, quick!' she heard Basil rap out a command, then a shutter seemed to click in her brain and she sagged limply in his arms as she slipped away into oblivion.

She had the curious sensation that she was floating through space, but she was forced back along a tunnel towards a pinpoint of light. When she reached it, it seemed to disintegate into a commanding voice ordering her to open her eyes, and she did so reluctantly.

'How do you feel now?' Basil was asking her.

'All right, I suppose,' she answered curiously. 'What happened?'

'You became a little over-excited.'

'What about?' she frowned, and when Basil did not reply at once, she slid her hands a little agitatedly over the sheets. The realisation that she was lying in a bed made her ask anxiously, 'Where am I?'

'You're in the clinic,' Basil told her in that same quiet tone he had used from the moment she had recovered consciousness.

'Did I have an accident?' she asked warily, not understanding.

'No, there was no accident.' There was a perturbed silence, then he asked carefully, 'Do you know who I am?'

'Of course I know who you are, silly,' she laughed lightly. 'You're Basil Vaughn and I'm Roxana Cunningham, and I'm not suffering from amnesia, if that's what you're thinking.'

'Then you know about the operation,' he seemed to sigh with relief.

'Operation?' she demanded at once, frighteningly alert for the first time. 'What operation?'

'*Your* operation.'

'But I haven't had an operation,' she argued, trying desperately to grasp the situation. 'What are you talking about?'

'I operated on you yesterday, Roxy,' Basil said, and he explained briefly what had occurred. 'Don't you remember?'

'No . . .' she frowned. 'It's absolutely fantastic news, of course, but . . . why can't I remember?'

'Don't upset yourself. It will all come back to you.'

'But I feel as though there's a dreadful blank in my memory, and . . .' She gripped his hands tightly. 'Basil, I'm frightened!'

'I'll ask Dr Gordon to take a look at you, and I'm certain he'll tell you, as I have, that there's nothing to be concerned about, and that your memory will return in time,' Basil assured her. 'It is, after all, only a partial lapse of memory.'

'The last thing I seem to remember quite clearly is when you dropped me off at my father's office,' she explained, making an effort to concentrate. 'I was worried about Noreen Butler, I know, and then I recall going up in the lift to my father's office, and then . . . nothing.'

'Noreen Butler was discharged from the clinic more than two months ago,' Basil stated, making her realise more fully the nightmarish situation which she now found herself in. 'Today is the seventh of July.'

'Oh, God!' she exclaimed in alarm. 'I've lived through more than two months of which I can't remember a thing.'

Basil's hands eased her agitated body back against the pillows. 'Just relax. You've suffered an emotionally traumatic experience, and you will eventually recall everything.'

'But *when*?' she demanded with breathless anxiety.

'I can't say, but don't try to force it,' he warned. 'Let it come naturally.'

Dr Gordon came to see Roxy as Basil had asked him

to, and she found him an understanding man with a soothing voice. It was partial amnesia, he confirmed Basil's diagnosis, and it was a temporary condition, but he could not tell her how long it would take for her memory to be restored to her.

'The most important thing is not to force it,' he instructed in that soothing voice that washed away her doubts and fears. 'Certain incidents, names, and places will eventually trigger off a spark of memory, and it will grow like a puzzle until all the pieces fit one into the other. The brain is the cleverest and the most sensitive part of the body, but occasionally, when something disturbing occurs, it closes certain doors and shuts out the memory of that incident which has affected you in a similar manner to shock. Consider this a time of healing and, when your conscious mind is ready once more to accept the facts which it now finds so unpalatable, your brain will release the information you require.'

Roxy did not pretend to understand entirely, but she found herself accepting his assurances and looking forward instead to the time when she would be able to see again.

It would be a slow process, Basil had warned, but she was content now to wait. Her father visited her twice a day until she was allowed to go home, and when Roxy stepped from the car she was greeted by a yelping Sheba who nearly knocked her down in her excitement.

'Welcome home,' her father said delightedly as he steadied her, and Roxy laughed happily as she knelt down and wrapped her arms about Sheba's furry body.

Beneath the woollen cap Roxy wore, her hair had started to grow, but, as she stroked Sheba's smooth coat, she smiled ruefully at the realisation that it would be a long time before her hair reached the length of Sheba's.

As the days passed and lengthened into weeks Roxy began to distinguish between light and dark, but she still made use of Sheba to guide her where she needed to go. Her excitement knew no bounds, however, when she awoke one morning to find she could recognise certain objects in her bedroom through the film of mist which still clouded her vision. A visit to Basil's consulting-rooms confirmed that it should not be long before she would have her vision restored totally.

A difficult period of adjustment lay ahead of her, Basil had warned, but she had never realised how difficult it would be until she actually experienced it. During the months following her operation there were times when she felt like a child learning all the fundamental things from the very beginning, such as controlling her balance in a crazy, tilting world, and relying on her eyes instead of her touch and sense of smell to define certain objects. Instead of enjoying the restoration of her sight, she found she was more often frustrated by it, and it took time to adjust herself to the things which had seemed so natural ten years ago.

There had been no joy in being able to choose her own clothes and, at first, she had been inclined to choose a vivid range of wild colours until she finally settled for something more subdued and in keeping with her nature. Learning to apply her make-up had been a hilarious experience, both for Maggie and herself. Being able to see had somehow robbed her hands of their deftness, and more often than not she had ended up with lipstick on her chin.

What Roxy had hated most was having to wear a

wig until her own hair had grown to a reasonable length, and six months passed, including the Christmas season, before she was able to discard the false hairpiece. Her own hair now lay in short, soft curls close to her head and, as Basil had promised her father, the scar left by the operation was not visible unless one searched for it.

Roxy studied herself in the mirror one evening after she had dressed herself with care to join her father for dinner downstairs. The face that stared back at her was the face of a woman, and no longer the childish face she had remembered with the smattering of freckles across the bridge of the small, straight nose. Her eyes could only be described as green, with mysterious hidden depths, and she stared into them searchingly, wondering what it was that lay hidden there even from herself. Her mouth was soft and full, with the slight suggestion of sensuality as if it had known the passion of a man's kisses. Had there been a man in her life during those two shuttered months? She rejected the idea at once and slid her criticial glance down the length of her figure. She had been a skinny, gangling twelve-year-old, but there was nothing skinny about her now, she decided, taking pleasure in looking at herself. She was slender, but the soft material of her cream-coloured evening gown accentuated the womanly curves of her long-limbed, shapely figure.

She was not unattractive, she thought, continuing her critical appraisal of herself. She was, in fact, more attractive than she had imagined, but she was still a stranger to herself. When she closed her eyes she felt familiar, but when she stared at herself in the mirror, it was like facing someone she had met once before; someone who looked vaguely familiar, but whom she could not place.

She went downstairs eventually, and slid her hand along the banister as she had always done. It was no longer for the purpose of guiding herself, but merely to form a definite association between the unfamiliarity of what she saw and the familiarity of touch. She still found that she relied heavily on her other senses, but Basil assured her that it would eventually diminish.

Theodore's eyes, so very like her own, smiled at her from across the dining-room when she walked in, and she went up to him where he sat at the head of the long oak table, and dropped a light kiss on to his grey head.

'You look tired,' she remarked, acquainting herself once again with the thin, lined features of this man who had aged so much over the years. 'Have you had a hectic day?'

'A mad day,' he confirmed, taking her hand in his when she sat down in her usual place at his left. 'Have you been out shopping again?'

She saw him take in the smooth lines of the dress she was wearing, and smiled. 'Do you like it?'

'Very sophisticated,' he nodded, staring at her appreciatively. 'It makes you look cool, confident, and poised.'

'Like that alabaster statue in the hall?' she teased, her eyes alight with amusement, and he tapped her cheek playfully with his fingers, but he was prevented from replying when their dinner was wheeled into the dining-room.

Her loss of memory had never been discussed during these months she had been recovering at home, and incidents which might have occurred during that passage of time she could not recall were never mentioned. She just wondered at times why they had so stoically avoided the subject, but coping with the miracle of being able to see again had been enough with which to occupy herself.

'What you need is a nice long holiday in the country,' Theodore told her after dinner when they had settled down with their coffee in the living-room where the cool evening breeze stirred the curtains at the french windows. 'I know of a place in the mountains where the air is fresh and the scenery is magnificent,' he added persuasively.

'I don't particularly want to leave home,' Roxy protested, absently caressing Sheba's silky ear.

Poor Sheba, Roxy thought. This beautiful golden labrador at her feet was still most perturbed at the change in her mistress, and at times she appeared quite bewildered and hurt at the knowledge that Roxy could do without her assistance.

'Roxy, my dear . . .' her father interrupted her thoughts. 'Perhaps you might find that hidden part of your memory in the peace and quiet of the mountains.'

Her smile faded and a frown appeared on her brow at the mention of that void in her life and, glancing at her father intently, she asked: 'Did anything unusual happen during that time I can't recall?'

'Why should you think anything unusual happened?' her father laughed, but he looked tense, and his laughter had been forced.

'Everyone has always studiously avoided discussing that period in my life,' she explained, her expression troubled.

'The reason for that is simple. Dr Gordon suggested that we don't force the issue while you're still convalescing,' Theodore tried to brush aside the matter. 'He said to wait until you displayed a natural curiosity.'

'I'm curious now,' she said, seating herself on the edge of her chair and holding her father's glance. 'Did anything happen that I should know about?'

Theodore shifted uncomfortably in his chair and cleared his throat. 'There was someone you became very attached to.'

'Was it a man?'

'Yes.'

'Was I in love with him?'' she asked, holding her breath.

Theodore nodded. 'I think so.'

'What was his name?'

'Marcus Fleming.'

The name bounced through Roxy's mind like a flat pebble bouncing across the water. It disturbed the surface of her memory, but before she could delve deeper, the impression had faded.

'Does his name bring anything to mind?' her father asked casually.

'No ... nothing at all,' she shook her head unhappily, 'but if I was in love with this man, as you say, then how could I have forgotten him so completely?'

'It will all come back to you eventually,' he assured her, getting up to close the french windows when the breeze became too strong.

She had been in love with someone; someone by the name of Marcus Fleming, and yet she could not remember a thing about him. She felt cheated somehow, and vaguely uneasy when she thought about it, but then a more disturbing thought came to mind.

'Why has he never been to see me?'

'When he paid you a visit in the clinic you absolutely refused to see him,' Theodore told her, returning to his chair. 'You could hardly blame him now for staying out of your way, could you?'

'I suppose not,' she agreed, pressing her fingers against her temples in an effort to remember. 'But if I loved him, why would I have refused to see him?'

'I'm afraid I can't tell you that,' he said, shaking his grey head as he stared at her thoughtfully for a moment, then he returned to the subject he had mentioned earlier. 'About that holiday in the mountains. Will you go if I make the necessary arrangements?'

Roxy stretched her shapely limbs out in front of her and leaned back lazily in her chair. Perhaps her father was right. It might be good for her to get away for a while and, setting aside her problems for the moment, she smiled into his anxious eyes. 'I think it would be nice to have a holiday in the mountains, but not for longer than two weeks.'

'Good!' he rubbed his hands together excitedly. 'A few weeks in the fresh country air will put the colour back into your cheeks.'

The arrangements were made swiftly, and Roxy went shopping for warmer clothes. It was late summer, but in the Drakensberg the air was inclined to be cool, she was told, and the nights could become decidedly chilly.

'Don't overdo things,' Basil warned when Roxy went for her final check-up, 'and don't expose your eyes as yet to glaring light. Wear your tinted glasses during the day until your eyes are stronger.'

Roxy observed him closely and it took a considerable effort on her part not to smile. Basil had behaved more like a mother hen fussing over her chick than a doctor attending a patient, and at times she had had the uneasy feeling that she meant more to him than just a friend and patient. He was older, too, than she had imagined, and his dark, springy hair was white against his temples. Lean, attractive, and distinguished were the adjectives which came to mind at that moment.

'I must admit, Roxy,' he interrupted her thoughts, 'I was petrified when you insisted that I perform the operation.'

'I can't imagine why I insisted you should attempt something you considered dangerous,' she smiled up into his grey eyes despite the fact that his confession had surprised her. 'I'm not sorry, though, and neither are you, I'm sure.'

'No, I'm not sorry. It was a miracle, and I'm grateful that I was the implement through which it could be performed.' His fingers caressed her cheek, then he withdrew his hand abruptly and pulled her to her feet. 'Come, your father is waiting for you, and I hope you enjoy your short holiday in the mountains.'

Had she glimpsed pain in Basil's eyes, or had it been her imagination? she wondered curiously when her father drove her home, but aloud she said: 'I wonder why Basil should have looked so unhappy when we said goodbye. Do you suppose he imagines I shan't want to help him in future at the clinic?'

Her father glanced at her quickly, and then away again. 'He's in love with you.'

Oh, lord, so that was it! she thought in dismay. Basil was in love with her, and she was supposedly in love with someone she could not even recall. Oh, *damn*! Why couldn't she remember!

She would have to learn to drive, Roxy decided on the Saturday during the long journey to the hotel in the Drakensberg, but for the present her father and Maggie were still quite happily acting as her chauffeur. They were booked into separate suites in the chalet-type hotel with a view overlooking the valley below, and they spent a relaxing weekend together before Theodore attempted the tiring drive home to Johannesburg.

Roxy opened the doors of her suite and stepped out on to the balcony which was bathed in sunshine. She felt lonely now that her father had left, and she leaned against the sturdy wooden railing as she let her glance travel appreciatively over the smooth lawns below her. To her left lay the tennis courts where several couples were enjoying a game before lunch, but only a few young men braved the cool water of the swimming pool.

A movement caught her eye, and she glanced towards the track leading higher up into the mountains. A man was striding along the path down to the hotel, his broad shoulders appearing broader in the dark blue windcheater, while the faded blue denims accentuated his lean hips and muscular thighs. She had seen him before, this tall man with the strong, rugged features, and short light-brown hair which looked deceptively fair in the sunlight. He had sat just two tables away from her father and herself at dinner the previous evening, and the piercing quality of his deep blue eyes had disturbed her intensely throughout the meal.

His sturdy climbing boots crunched on the gravel below her moments later, and then, suddenly, he paused and looked up. Startled into immobility, she found herself staring helplessly down into his disturbing eyes like someone hypnotised, and the colour in her cheeks deepened when his stern mouth relaxed into a faintly mocking smile before he walked on and disappeared into the hotel.

Roxy was surprised to find that she was shaking when she entered her suite and closed the doors behind her. There was something about that man that frightened her, and she was beginning to regret that she had agreed to come away on her own for two weeks.

She saw him again at lunch, and felt certain that he had deliberately seated himself at the table in a position where he would face her. Damn the man! she thought angrily. Judging by that faintly mocking smile that hovered about his mouth, he was fully aware of the alarming effect he was having on her, and he was obviously enjoying it. Damn him!

At dinner that evening she seated herself with her back to him, but that made the situation considerably worse when she felt his eyes boring into her back, and she was finally forced to return to her suite without doing justice to the superb meal.

Later that evening, when she slipped into her coat and went for a stroll in the well-lit grounds of the hotel, *he* was there as well. He was leaning against a tree with his hands thrust deep into the pockets of his corduroy pants, and he looked suddenly as if he had been waiting there for her to join him. She paused abruptly in her stride when she saw him incline his head in a brief, mocking greeting, then she swung away in the opposite direction and quickened her pace. To her dismay, he followed her, but he made no effort to catch up with her, and merely remained some distance behind her. He was really a most infuriating man, she thought when her skin began to crawl and, relinquishing the effort to appear casual, she almost sprinted back to the hotel and went upstairs to closet herself in her suite.

She went to bed shortly after ten, but she could not sleep, and it was almost midnight when a heavy step on the balcony outside her window made her get out of bed and draw the curtain aside. It was that man again, she discovered, and he was leaning with his hands on the wooden railings while he stared out across the star-studded valley with the jutting mountains silhouetted against the night sky in the distance. Roxy stood there observing him, curiosity overcoming her wariness. Who and what was he? she wondered frowningly. And why did his presence fill her with such nervous dread? He turned his head suddenly, as if he sensed that he was being observed, and she drew back sharply, holding her breath, but he could not see her, of course, behind the heavy lace at the window of her darkened room.

He stared directly at her window for long seconds until she felt certain that, even though he could not see her, he must surely hear the heavy thudding of her heart, then she saw him push a hand through his hair as if he had become agitated about something. He stared out into the darkness a moment longer, then he turned and, to her horror, she discovered that he had been booked into the suite next to her own. She let the curtain fall back into place and went back to bed, but it was a long time before she fell asleep.

After breakfast the following morning, Roxy changed into a warm pair of slacks, sturdy, comfortable walking shoes, and a red anorak which she put on over her knitted sweater and zipped up to beneath her chin. The path into the mountain was quite safe, she had been informed by the desk clerk, and that was where she intended going.

It was a steady upward climb, but she took it in easy stages, resting whenever she needed to, and drinking in the spectacular scenery like someone who had thirsted for it a long time. She had never before seen mountains so ruggedly majestic, nor valleys so deep and lush, she decided as she paused once more to draw breath, then she turned to look back the way she had come, and her heart lurched like a frightened bird in her breast. She did not need to be clairvoyant to know who was striding up along the track below her, and he was gaining steadily on her too. It was that man again, and, determined to keep away from him, she walked on, climbing higher and higher until her breath rasped in her pulsating throat, and her aching limbs forced her to rest on a rock beneath a shady tree. He had gained on her, she noticed with a feeling of dread, and within a few short minutes she knew he would reach her, but tiredness overwhelmed her, and left her with no way of avoiding this meeting.

She leaned back against the stem of the tree, pushed her tinted glasses up on to her head, and closed her eyes as she waited for his arrival with a feeling close to peril. She sat there, wanting to run, yet too tired to do so as she listened to his footsteps coming determinedly closer. She opened her eyes at length to see him standing a little distance away from her, and he was surveying her with a curious mixture of triumph and mockery in his eyes. Instead of the blue windcheater and denims he had worn the day before, he was wearing a brown leather jacket and khaki pants, and panic had a stranglehold on her throat when he lessened the distance between them to tower over her. His intensely blue eyes travelled over her slowly and systematically, leaving her with the alarming sensation that she had been stripped naked and, lowering her glasses on to her nose, she jumped to her feet, intent upon returning the way she had come.

'If you climb a little higher you'll have a magnificent view of the mountains and the valleys,' his voice stopped her. It was deep with a resonant timbre, and hauntingly familiar. She turned to stare at him, her eyes wide and searching behind the tinted lenses, then the vague memory receded with equal swiftness into that cloistered section of her mind.

'Follow me,' he said, and she followed as if she no longer had a will of her own.

He kept to the track for a while, then he veered off to the left, and she found herself following him across a much rougher terrain. Before she could become tired or nervous, however, she found herself on a plateau of sorts, and looking out across the rugged ridge of mountains which seemed to reach from the deep, gorging valleys up towards the sky where the jutting peaks disappeared amongst the clouds.

Roxy felt small and insignificant when she sat down on the flat rock behind her. For endless minutes she savoured the breathtaking view which seemed to continue as far as the eye could see, but then she became aware of the presence of that disturbing man who stood admiring the view a little distance away from her.

CHAPTER EIGHT

THE cold breeze whipped colour into Roxy's cheeks, and penetrated her clothes so that she shivered and wrapped her arms about herself protectively. Her icy hands felt numb, and she could no longer feel her toes in her shoes when her companion swung his rucksack off his shoulders and seated himself beside her on the rock.

'It provides one with a sense of freedom and a great deal of humility to be up here where the earth and the sky seem to meet,' he remarked conversationally while he undid the rucksack, but she kept her face averted, and said nothing. 'Have you ever seen anything so beautiful?' he asked.

She shook her head, and said through clenched teeth, 'No.'

'Coffee?' Something touched her hand and she turned her head sharply to see the mug he held out towards her. When she made no move to accept it, he said impatiently, 'Go on, take it.'

She took the mug from him then, and wrapped her cold hands about it in order to warm them while she watched him take a second mug from his rucksack to fill it with coffee from a small flask. He had strong, well-shaped hands, she noticed, and the fingernails were short and clean, suggesting that his work, whatever it was, was not of a manual kind. He returned the flask to his rucksack before picking up the mug he had placed on the rock beside him and, as he did so, their eyes met.

Roxy coloured, but she did not look away as she asked with some urgency, 'Who *are* you?'

'James Allen,' he smiled a little twistedly. 'And you're Roxana Cunningham.'

She drew a startled breath. 'Who told you that?'

'I asked at the reception desk,' he said matter-of-factly, then he gestured abruptly towards the mug she clasped between her hands. 'Drink that coffee. It will warm you up a little before we start the long walk down to the hotel.'

Roxy obeyed him in silence, but her mind was running riot. *James Allen.* He did not look like a James Allen. He was too vitally masculine to be saddled with an ordinary name like that. There was in his voice and manner that indefinable thread of steel, an arrogance in the way he held his head, and a determination in the square set of his jaw. She was suddenly overcome by the strangest desire to touch him, but she pulled herself together at once, and placed her empty mug beside the rucksack at his feet.

Going down was not so easy. She was unused to such strenuous exertion, and her legs felt weak and shaky beneath her. She caught the toe of her shoe on a protruding rock in an unguarded moment, and slipped as she tried to regain her balance, but James Allen turned at that moment and caught her deftly before she could injure herself.

She clutched wildly at the muscled arms beneath the leather jacket, but it felt as though she had been wired up to an electrical unit when her body made contact with his. Her nerve-ends vibrated as if from a hidden energy source, and her pulse became erratic when, instead of releasing her, his arm tightened about her waist. With his free hand he removed her tinted glasses and stared down into her wide, frightened eyes.

'You have lovely eyes, Roxana Cunningham,' he said, his voice low, vibrant and disturbing. 'They're as green as the valleys below us, with elusive and mysterious depths that would encourage any man to probe deeper.'

'Let me go,' she whispered hoarsely, trying to free herself, but his arm merely tightened about her so that his hard thighs pressed against her own.

'You're afraid of me.'

It was a statement, not a question and, as she fought to control the tremors that shook through her, she said stiffly, 'I don't know you.'

'You *will* eventually,' he assured her with a confidence that alarmed her further, then he slipped her tinted glasses back on to her nose and released her.

'Come,' he said abruptly, taking her arm firmly in his hand. 'We haven't much further to go.'

Roxy felt as though she had been caught up in a nightmare, and when she finally reached the safety of her suite in the hotel, she was mentally and physically exhausted. She soaked herself in a hot bath to ease the stiffness from her limbs, and tried not to think, but her mind continued to pivot around those moments she had stood in the circle of his arm. The most frightening thing about it had been that uncanny sense of belonging she had experienced, and it unnerved her even now to think of it. There had to be some practical and logical explanation for what she had felt, she decided when she eventually climbed out of the bath and dried herself vigorously with the towel. The exertion of walking up the mountain had been too much for her, she told herself at last, and in her weakened state she had imagined something that was not there.

She did not go down to lunch, however, and decided to play safe by having something sent up to her. She did not want to meet James Allen again; not so soon, at least, after their encounter on the mountain, so she remained in her suite that afternoon and tried to relax. She would feel differently when she met him again, but preferably it would be to her advantage to stay out of his way in future.

She steeled herself when she went down to dinner that evening, but that did not prevent her heart from leaping crazily in her breast when she saw him seated at the table close to hers. They acknowledged each other's presence with a brief nod, and she placed her order with the waiter who hovered politely in attendance. She might as well have been eating sawdust, she told herself eventually as she forced the food down her throat. James Allen was sitting two tables away from her drinking his coffee, and she was acutely conscious of every move he made, and every gesture of those strong, well-shaped hands. He observed her intently and quite openly and, although she tried to ignore the fact, her hands were trembling to the extent that she found it increasingly difficult to hold her knife and fork properly.

He rose to his feet eventually, but her relief was shortlived when he approached her table and pulled out the chair opposite her.

'May I join you?' he asked, his eyes mocking her.

'I can't stop you, I suppose,' she said sarcastically as she watched him seat himself.

'Why be so determined to be unfriendly?'

'I prefer to be on my own.'

'Ah!' he said, his eyebrows rising in sardonic amusement. 'Like Greta Garbo, the lady wants to be left alone.'

Angry frustration surged through her and, dropping her knife and fork on to her plate, she pushed back her chair and rose to her feet. 'Excuse me.'

'You haven't finished your dinner,' he remarked accusingly, getting to his feet with animal-like swiftness and following her from the dining-room.

'I'm not hungry,' she flung at him across her shoulder as she pushed her way through the swing doors into the foyer, but when strong fingers latched on to her wrist she swung round to face him and cried out furiously, 'Why can't you leave me alone?'

His eyes were hooded as they slid over her slender form in the cinnamon-coloured jersey-cloth dress, then he smiled that mocking smile she was beginning to hate intensely. 'There's a moon outside, and you're dressed warm enough, so let's go for a walk.'

He literally dragged her from the building before

she could utter a protest, and she practically had to run to keep up with his long-legged strides.

'You have a nerve, treating me like this!' she accused breathlessly when they reached a secluded section of the grounds.

'The fresh air will cool your temper,' he laughed briefly, shortening his strides to accommodate her, but his laughter had touched a sensitive chord in her brain, and it unleashed a fury that made her shake with the force of it.

'You're an overbearing, pompous——!'

The words became strangled in her throat as he swung her round into his arms, and her anger seemed to drain from her when she found herself staring up into his rugged, shadowy face. The scent of his spicy, masculine cologne was in her nostrils, stirring her senses until she felt again that peculiar sensation of belonging. She wanted to free herself, but her mind and her body had become oddly retarded as she stood there staring up at him dumbly and helplessly.

'You were saying, Roxana?' he mocked her, but, when she remained silent, he lowered his head and sought her lips with his own.

The pressure of his mouth against hers was light but persistent, and, paralysed by a force far stronger than she had ever encountered, she offered no resistance. Encouraged by her stillness in his arms, his kisses became sensually arousing, and she found herself responding with a wild abandon of which she felt secretly ashamed, but which she could do nothing about at that moment as she clung to him weakly.

His mouth left hers at last to slide across her throat, and to probe the sensitive areas with an expertise that made her tremble against him as her emotions soared to incredible heights, but she came to her senses with humiliating swiftness when his hands slid upwards from her hips to her breasts.

She could not allow a total stranger such familiarities and, thrusting him from her, she cried chokingly, 'This is madness! I hardly know you!'

'But it feels as though we have known each other for a very long time.'

He spoke those words as if he had access to every thought that flashed through her mind, and she backed away from him in fear. 'Who *are* you?'

'You've asked me that before, and I've told you.' He bowed slightly in her direction. 'James Allen is the name, and I'm at your service.'

She stared up into his face, but the darkness unfortunately hid his expression from her. She had to get away, she told herself; away from this man who had the power to change her into someone she could hardly recognise as herself, and away from the intimacy of this shadowy niche in the gardens.

'I'd like to go up to my room,' she said stiffly, turning from him as she spoke.

'I'll take you up.'

'No!' she exclaimed sharply as he fell into step beside her. 'I'm perfectly capable of finding my own way.'

'I'll go no further than the door to your suite,' he assured her with an undertone of mockery in his deep voice. 'You have my word on that.'

Roxy lapsed into an exasperated silence, and made no further effort to stop him accompanying her. She did not speak, and neither did he as they entered the hotel, crossed the foyer, and climbed up the curved staircase, but her heart was beating hard and fast against her ribs when they walked along the thickly carpeted passage towards her suite. At her door he paused, held out a hand for her key, and inserted it in the lock. The door swung open, and he switched on the light, then he dropped the key into her outstretched palm and stepped back.

'Goodnight, Miss Cunningham,' he said tersely, then he turned his back on her and continued down the passage towards his own suite.

Roxy stared at that broad, formidable back with a perplexed expression in her eyes. For one mad instant she had a crazy desire to run after him, then she backed into her suite and closed the door quickly to lean against it heavily.

'Am I going mad?' she wondered frantically. What must he think of her? She hardly knew him, and yet she had allowed him to kiss her with a passionate intimacy to which she had responded shockingly.

Bewildering as it may have seemed to her, she knew that what had happened to her out there in the hotel gardens was something she had known before. But when—and more specifically—with whom? Marcus Fleming? The name her father had mentioned came to mind, but something within her recoiled from the very idea. No, it could not have been him.

Other arms had held her before, and other lips had kissed her in that passionate way, but surely, if it had been this Marcus Fleming her father had mentioned, his name would have stirred some chord in her sluggish memory?

She went to bed, but it was a long time before she slept, and then her dreams were filled with the most disturbing incidents. She was lying on soft grass, and she was blind once more. James Allen was bending over her, and she was exploring his lean, rugged features with her fingertips while he murmured something to her in that low, vibrating voice. He kissed her

eventually with a passion to which she responded
without reserve, then something frightening happened, and he was torn from her arms as if by a great
gust of wind. She cried out in despair, and awoke with
a thudding heart to find that it was morning. Her body
was wet with perspiration, and she was shaking uncontrollably as she glanced about her guardedly,
almost as if she expected to find James Allen there in
the room with her, then she threw back the bedclothes
with an angry exclamation on her lips, and went
through to the bathroom to run her bath water.

When she went down to breakfast an hour later, she
felt nervous at the prospect of meeting the man who
had featured so prominently in her dreams, but he was
not at his usual table and, struggling with a mixture of
relief and disappointment, she ate her breakfast
quickly before returning to her suite to collect her
fleece-lined jacket.

The air was cool despite the fact that the sun was
shining, and she went for a long walk down into the
valley until she found a quiet spot beside a little
stream where she could rest for a while and think
things over while she took in the panoramic beauty of
her surroundings. She was surrounded by tall cycad,
sagewood and cypress trees which were casting long
shadows across the dew-bedecked earth sparkling in
the early morning sun.

Roxy sat down on a dry, grassy patch, leaning with
her back against the gnarled stem of an old tree as she
watched the rippling stream run swiftly from its
source somewhere in the mountains down into the
valley below. The water was crystal clear, and refresh-
ing to drink, she discovered when she leaned forward
to scoop a handful to her mouth, then she sat back
once more and closed her eyes for a moment behind

the tinted lenses of her glasses. The air was fresh and
sweet, and she drew it deeply into her lungs. Nature
had been left undisturbed in this mountainous area,
and the indigenous plants grew wild and free and pro-
tected from the destruction of human hands.

'Peaceful, isn't it?' a voice pierced the stillness, and
she scrambled to her feet nervously to find James
Allen standing a little distance from her, his feet
planted firmly apart, and his thumbs hooked into the
broad leather belt that hugged his denims to his lean
hips.

'Until this moment, yes,' she agreed with angry sarcasm as her agitated glance swept higher to take in the
long-sleeved denim shirt that seemed to fit too tightly
across his broad chest, but her eyes lingered on the
strong, sun-browned neck, and the proud head tilted
at an arrogant, faintly mocking angle.

'You find my presence disturbing, then?' he asked
with a hint of laughter in his voice as he lessened the
distance between them.

'Why won't you leave me alone?' she cried, resorting to anger as a result of her inability to find an explanation for her physical reaction to this man.

'Do I have such an unpresentable appearance that
you can't stand me near you?' he demanded, standing
so close to her now that she had to raise her head to
look a long way up at him, and she saw his mouth
twist into a suggestion of a smile. 'There's no third eye
in the middle of my forehead, is there?'

'No,' she laughed before she was able to prevent
herself. 'And you don't have a broken nose, or buck
teeth either, but——'

She drew a sharp breath and felt the colour drain
from her face. She had been on achingly familiar
ground, but now, as she grasped at the memory, it
faded with infuriating swiftness, and was gone.

'Sit down,' said James, taking her by the shoulders and forcing her down on to the soft ground so that she leaned with her back against the tree once more. His eyes searched her face intently, then he said: 'You've gone quite pale.'

'I—I'm sorry,' she said weakly, pressing her fingers against her throbbing temples in an effort to remember. 'It was something you said, and the way I replied. It all sounded so familiar—as if I'd heard it somewhere before, but——'

She bit her lip in concentration, but nothing emerged from those hidden shadows in her mind, and her hands fell limply into her lap as she closed her eyes and leaned her head back against the tree trunk.

'It happens sometimes,' James Allen was saying. 'Things, certain incidents, become vague in one's mind.'

She opened her eyes suddenly to stare at him. He must think her mad, she thought a little hysterically as her glance rested on that strong yet sensuous mouth, and the square, determined jaw. She felt an intense desire to touch him; it rose from deep within her until her fingertips tingled with a strange longing that frightened her.

'I think I'd better get back to the hotel,' she said unsteadily, but a heavy hand came down on to her shoulder, forcing her to remain where she was.

'Don't go yet,' he instructed. 'Rest a while longer.'

She shrank from the touch of his hand, and he removed it at once, but he remained seated close to her, propping himself up with one hand while the other arm rested on his raised knee. His nearness stirred her senses in an oddly familiar way, and she stared at him thoughtfully, her eyes searching, while her mind probed relentlessly and without success into that blank period of her life.

'Why do I have the feeling that I know you?' she heard herself question him at last.

'Perhaps we knew each other in another lifetime.'

'That's silly,' she laughed jerkily. 'I don't believe in reincarnation.'

He shrugged and stared out across the stream, giving her the opportunity to study his strong profile. He was not a man to be trifled with, she knew this somehow, and she knew, too, that he was a man who nearly always succeeded in getting what he wanted. He turned his head, then, and their eyes met, sending a shiver of shock along her receptive nerves. The blueness of his eyes intensified, and she stared, fascinated, when the pupils enlarged as if with some inner emotion.

'What do you see when you look at me like that, Roxana Cunningham?' he enquired softly, and the sheer force of his masculinity held her spellbound for interminable seconds before she could free herself.

'I can see that it's time I returned to the hotel,' she said, the huskiness in her voice more pronounced as a result of her inner turmoil.

'You don't have to fear me.' His heavy hand on her shoulder once again prevented her from rising. 'I don't want to hurt you.'

I don't want to hurt you. Those words echoed through her mind like a ghost from the past, and she shivered involuntarily.

'Someone else said that to me once, and——'

'You were hurt?' he questioned when she paused abruptly.

'I think so. I—I can't remember.'

He smiled faintly. 'There are many things you don't remember.'

'Why do you say that?' she asked sharply, instantly on the defensive.

'I said something a few minutes ago that made you

think of something else you couldn't remember,' he explained in an unperturbed manner.

'I've suffered a partial lapse of memory,' she told him, not really knowing why she should confide in him. 'There's a part of my life I can't remember at all, and I'm left with about ten blank weeks I'm unable to fill.'

'Is it important that you should remember?'

'I have a feeling that it is.' She frowned and fingered the pleat in her slacks. 'My father told me that there'd been someone—someone I——'

'Someone you cared about?' James filled in for her when she paused abruptly.

'Yes,' she admitted, her cheeks growing warm under his scrutiny.

'And you can't remember him at all?'

She shook her head. 'No, I'm afraid I can't.'

'Do you really want to remember?'

'I—I don't know.' She felt the nerves tighten at the pit of her stomach, and she replied with inherent honesty, 'If I have to analyse myself, I think I'll find I'm a little afraid to remember.'

'So you've decided to keep that part of your life locked away in your mind because you're afraid to face whatever it is that happened during that time you can't remember.'

His scornful accusation stung her, and she jumped to her feet in a fury. 'Don't say it like that! I didn't deliberately shut that period out of my mind, so what right have you to sit there and pass judgment on me!'

He got to his feet and towered over her suddenly, his hands gripping her shoulders and shaking her slightly. 'I wasn't judging you, you little spitfire.'

'I don't know why I actually bothered talking to you,' she spat out the words. 'You're a complete stranger to me, and I would prefer to keep it that way.'

'Well, I don't!' he assured her harshly and, before

she could suspect his intentions, she was draped across one hard arm and kissed with a thoroughness that left her trembling and shaken. 'That's something you're not going to forget in a hurry.'

He turned on the heel of his suede boots and walked away, leaving her standing there with her back pressed hard against the steam of the cycad, and her breath coming unevenly over parted, bruised lips. Her troubled eyes followed his tall, broad-shouldered figure until he was out of sight, then she struggled with the curious desire to weep. Somewhere within her there was a deep sorrow; a regret, as if something had been left undone, and it filled her with a yearning that seemed to tear away at her insides. James Allen was to blame for arousing these feelings in her, and she was beginning to fear that, mentally and physically, she would become enslaved by a man she had met for the first time barely a few days ago. If it had happened to someone else she would have laughed scornfully at the whole idea of such an instant attraction, but it was happening to *her*, and it was dangerously real.

It frightened her, this attraction for a man she hardly knew, but it was there every time they met; the awareness of his enigmatic presence, the magnetism that drew her to him relentlessly like a moth to a flame, and his masculine vitality which made her so disturbingly aware of her femininity. His piercing blue eyes had the power to stir her senses, while his touch ignited a fire in her veins and, humiliating though it might seem to her at that moment, deep down she wanted his touch with an aching need she could not assuage. That was the reason she feared him so much. She was afraid of what he could do to her, but, moreover, she was afraid of what he might make *her* do.

'Oh, God!' she groaned, burying her white face in her trembling hands. 'What's happening to me!'

There was no answer forthcoming; no logical explanation she could offer herself, and the effort of trying to understand merely succeeded in exhausting her.

She once again decided to have lunch sent up to her suite that day, and afterwards she slept for almost two hours before awaking relaxed and free of a great deal of the tension which had plagued her. She showered and changed into a satin, apricot-coloured evening dress with wide sleeves. It was a dress she had brought with the intention of wearing on special occasions, but nothing special was about to happen, she decided, so she might as well indulge in a little fantasy of her own. She took care over her make-up, and brushed her short hair until it curled softly about her ears. It would be a long time before her hair reached the length it had been before her operation, she thought with a grimace, but she supposed she should not complain.

With time to spare before going down to dinner, she stepped out on to the balcony for a breath of fresh air. The sun had set swiftly to shroud the earth in darkness, and she felt the peace of her surroundings settle about her like a soft, protective cloak as she leaned against the railing and stared up at the starlit sky.

It was a miracle that she could see; that she could watch the stars flickering brightly in the velvety sky as she had done so often as a child, and gratitude flooded her being and brought tears to her eyes.

She had no idea how long she had stood there, enmeshed in her own thoughts, but her peace was finally disturbed when she sensed that she was no longer alone, and she turned to see James Allen observing her from the darkened doorway of his suite. Her pulse fluttered, stilled, and fluttered again as they faced each other across the silent balcony. She wanted to turn away, but she couldn't, and for a time nothing moved except the soft mountain breeze stirring the folds of her dress about her legs.

'Come here, Roxy.'

It was a command, quietly spoken, but decisive, and her limbs obeyed with a will of their own, taking her into his arms as if she belonged there. A glimmer of a smile hovered on his shadowed features, then his mouth brushed hers tantalisingly until the final shred of her restraint crumbled, and her lips parted hungrily for his kiss.

Lost in the exciting intimacy of this moment, she was only vaguely conscious of being drawn into his suite, but she did not care. She heard the door close with a soft 'click', then his hands were moulding her softness against the hard length of his body, and a wild response clamoured through her that left her clinging to him weakly. She seemed to come alive beneath those clever hands, and she moaned softly as his mouth brushed across her eyes, her cheek, and her throat before seeking her willing lips once more. It all seemed so achingly familiar, and all at once a memory was struggling to the forefront of her brain.

'Wait . . . please!' she begged hoarsely, holding him off with her palms pressed flat against his chest, and the warmth of his skin through the fine linen of his shirt sent an odd sensation rippling through her as she gasped, 'There's—there's something I *must* remember. I *must*!'

'Don't force it, Roxana,' he said, releasing her and flicking a switch against the wall behind him so that she stood blinking with momentary blindness in the sharp light that flooded the room so unexpectedly.

'Stop calling me Roxana!' she cried agitatedly, trying to grasp the vague memory which was slipping so swiftly away from her. 'You called me Roxy a few minutes ago.'

A smile touched his mouth. 'Why don't you call me James?'

'James,' she repeated thoughtfully, tilting her head up at him and relinquishing the effort to remember. 'It doesn't suit you somehow.'

'My name doesn't matter,' he gestured abruptly with an expressive hand. 'What does matter is that I would like to help you.'

'Help me?' She stared at him incredulously, taking in the height and breadth of him in the dark, impeccably tailored suit. 'Did you say you want to help me?'

'I want to help you remember that part of your life which you've locked away somewhere in the recesses of your mind.'

There was absolute silence while she considered his amazing statement, then she asked suspiciously, 'And how do you propose to do that?'

'Does it matter which methods I use?' His compelling eyes held hers captive while his fingers brushed against her cheek in a casual caress. 'Trust me.'

Trust him? Could she trust him? Could she trust *herself*? Shame sent a hot wave of colour surging into her cheeks when she thought of how willingly she had gone into his arms a few minutes ago to return his kisses with a passion which had been almost frightening in its intensity.

She lowered her eyes and turned away from his disturbing touch. 'I don't really know you.'

'Then allow yourself to get to know me,' he insisted,

coming up behind her so that she could feel his breath stirring her hair. 'That shouldn't be too difficult, judging by the way you react to my kisses.'

Her colour deepened with embarrassment, and her fingers tightened about her sequinned purse. 'Why should you want to help me?'

'I like the colour of your eyes.'

'Don't be silly,' she laughed nervously, moving away from him towards the door leading out on to the balcony.

She had to get away, she thought frantically. She had to get away from this man who succeeded in confusing her more each time they met.

He made no effort to prevent her from leaving, but when her fingers touched the cold metal of the door handle he said: 'I've ordered dinner for two to be served here in my suite.'

Her hand trembled and tightened on the handle as she turned to face him, her movements slow and her eyes wary. 'Is this an invitation?'

He shook his head slightly and smiled that mocking smile she was beginning to associate with him. 'It's an order.'

'And if I refuse?'

'Then a perfectly good meal will go to waste.' Their glances met sparringly during the ensuing silence while she tried to decide what to do, then he came towards her and placed his hands lightly on her rigid shoulders. 'Relax,' he said, drawing her away from the door and further into the room which was furnished similarly to her own small lounge in the suite next to his. 'I'm really quite harmless,' he added reassuringly.

As harmless as a hunting leopard on the prowl, yes, she thought cynically as she lowered her taut body on to the padded leather armchair he had indicated. She felt tonguetied and nervous, and totally incapable of thinking of anything sensible to say. She was conscious of his tall, muscular figure seated in the chair opposite her own, and of those intensely blue eyes that never left her in peace. She was conscious, too, of her own physical awareness of him, of her heightened colour, and her quickening pulse rate. This man was a virtual stranger to her, but he held a fatal attraction for her, and here she was alone with him in his suite and about to share a meal with him. It smacked of intimacy and as her senses stirred, her mind warned her to leave at once while she still had the opportunity to do so, and the will to obey.

Her intentions were thwarted by a knock at the door, and James rose to his feet to admit a waiter wheeling a trolley. The small circular table close to the electric fire was set deftly and swiftly, a ten-Rand note exchanged hands, and then they were left alone once more.

Roxy felt herself go rigid and tense with nerves, and her eyes widened when she saw James remove a bottle of champagne from the ice and begin to undo the silver wrapper. Moments later she jumped nervously at the sound of the cork popping, and then a glass of bubbling liquid was placed in her trembling hand.

He touched the side of her glass with his own before raising it to his lips. 'To the future.'

'To the future,' she echoed unsteadily, wondering just what the future held in store for her, and longing suddenly for the familiarity and safety of her home in Johannesburg.

CHAPTER NINE

Roxy had been nervous of being alone with James in his suite, but he had kept up an interesting stream of conversation while they had eaten the excellent meal he had ordered. They had started off with shrimp cocktails, and a creamy vegetable soup which had been followed by chicken scallops in cream, fresh tomatoes stuffed with rice and cheese, and small roast potatoes. After the fruity dessert and coffee, the waiter had returned to remove the trolley of dishes, and then Roxy was again left alone with James. He gestured her on to the small sofa, and she sat down warily, her body taut and her palms damp as she watched him shed his jacket and tie.

'For God's sake, Roxy, I wish you'd relax!' he exclaimed harshly, his eyes raking over her in a derisive manner. 'I have no intention of dragging you into my bedroom to rape you.'

'I never thought anything of the kind,' she protested hotly, lowering her eyes when guilt stained her cheeks.

'Didn't you?' he demanded, and her cheeks grew warmer beneath his mocking gaze.

'All right, so I did!' she admitted at last. 'How am I expected to know what you have in mind for me?'

'I might try seducing you, but rape isn't in my line at all.'

There was a hint of sensuality in the smile that curved his strong mouth, and an inexplicable shiver of fear made her get hurriedly to her feet.

'I think I'd better go.'

'Sit down!' His voice had the effect of a whiplash, making her obey at once, and moments later he was extending a glass of champagne towards her. 'Drink this,' he ordered.

'Are you trying to make me drunk?' she asked suspiciously, realising that it would be her third glass of champagne within the space of an hour.

'I'm trying to help you relax,' he stated calmly as he picked up his own glass and seated himself beside her.

The sofa was small, and when his thigh touched hers she altered her position abruptly. 'How do you expect me to relax when you speak of rape and seduction?'

'I've already told you that rape isn't in my line,' he smiled at her mockingly over the rim of his glass. 'And I've always made it my policy never to seduce a woman unless she's seventy-five per cent willing.'

Roxy almost choked on a mouthful of champagne. 'Is that confession supposed to make me relax?'

'Why not?' He placed his arm along the back of the sofa behind her shoulders, and she stiffened in alarm when she felt his fingers caress the nape of her neck. 'At the moment you're scared frigid, which means that you register nil on the percentage scale.'

He was mocking her, she knew, but at that moment she was too busy controlling her wayward emotions to care. She took a second mouthful of champagne to steady herself, and tried to ignore those caressing fingers, but she could not ignore the sensations that shivered along her receptive nerves.

'Do you seduce every woman you meet?' she asked with a touch of cynicism, shifting her position carefully to avoid his persistent, disturbing touch.

'Yes,' he leered at her wickedly. 'I'm a sexual maniac.'

'Don't be ridiculous!' she muttered angrily, but for some reason she cowered away from him inwardly.

'A ridiculous question deserves a ridiculous answer,' he said abruptly, draining his glass and placing it on the low table beside the sofa.

There was an awkward silence which she tried to fill by sipping casually at the remainder of her drink, but when he did not speak she said apologetically, 'I'm sorry.'

'So am I,' said James, removing her glass from her cold fingers and placing it on the table beside his own. 'I think I would have enjoyed seducing you.'

This conversation had gone far enough, Roxy decided, attempting to get up, but his arm shot out, brushing against her breasts as he barred her way and forced her back into her seat. Her pulses leapt at his unexpected nearness, and the grim expression on his ruggedly handsome features filled her with dread.

'Please let me go,' she breathed nervously.

'Not until we've reached a firm understanding about each other,' he stated decisively, his hand gripping her shoulder so tightly that she winced inwardly. 'I intend helping you to regain your memory of those missing weeks,' he said through his teeth, 'and when I've done that you can tell me to stay, or get the hell out of your life.'

Her eyes widened with surprise and suspicion. 'And what do you hope to gain from that?'

He smiled suddenly, his hand caressing rather than bruising her. 'That, Roxy, depends entirely on yourself.'

'You mean it depends on whether I decide to get into bed with you or not,' she snapped angrily.

'You have a one-track mind,' he laughed briefly.

'Whose fault is that?'

'Not entirely mine, I assure you.' His hand was at

her throat, his thumb forcing her chin up so that she had no option but to meet his compelling gaze. 'I don't deny that I find you desirable, but I shan't force you to do anything you don't want to.'

His eyes probed hers, then shifted lower to her soft, pink mouth, and she quivered like a frightened animal in his hold. 'Please ... I must go. Thank you for a lovely dinner, but——'

His mouth silenced hers with a gentle force that drove her lips apart, and she struggled against him wildly, but her efforts were ineffectual as he drew her down on to the sofa and held her there with the hard pressure of his body. Her resistance finally crumbled as ecstatic emotions soared through her slender, trembling form to rise to a wild crescendo beneath the expertise of his lips and hands, but deep within her a memory stirred, leaving her with the distinct impression that this had happened to her before, and then, just as now, she had been driven to the very edge of desire.

James raised his head suddenly, and there was a gleam of mockery in his eyes as he drew away from her slightly. 'You're moving up fast on that percentage scale towards the seduction level.'

Her dulled mind did not grasp at once what he was referring to, but when it did her flushed cheeks went a deeper red as she thrust him from her and jumped to her feet.

'You're hateful!' she cried chokingly, picking up her purse and striding towards the door leading out on to the balcony with as much dignity as she could summon in her humiliation.

'Goodnight, Roxana Cunningham,' his mocking laughter followed her. 'Reserve a little space for me in your dreams.'

'I shall do nothing of the kind!' she snapped furiously as she wrenched open the door. 'Goodnight!'

The icy night air cooled her hot cheeks before she entered her suite and locked the door behind her. What madness had possessed her to submit to his lovemaking? she wondered angrily, sinking into a chair in the darkened room and burying her face in her hands. She recalled that fleeting memory she had experienced in his arms, and wondered why she should have imagined that something like that had happened to her once before. The thought perturbed her, but when that familiar throbbing headache started pounding against her temples she had to give up the effort of trying to remember. It was always the same, this wall of pain she encountered when she tried to delve into the hidden recesses of her mind.

James had stated that he wanted to help her, but his reasons for wanting to do this remained obscure to her. Why should he, a stranger, want to help her in any way, and with what purpose in mind? She tried to find an explanation for it, but failed, and was left instead with the gnawing suspicion that his motives might possibly not be as honourable as he had wished her to believe.

She was perhaps being foolish, she told herself when she went to bed, but so many things confused and bewildered her lately. During those long years of not being able to see, her memory had served her like a guiding, perceptive light within her, but the restoration of her sight had wiped out a part of her memory, and that light inside her had somehow been extinguished.

Roxy went down to breakfast early the following morning, and afterwards she decided to go for a long walk. It was a warm morning, and the hill she climbed was ablaze with colour as the wild flowers opened up their petals towards the sun. The wonder of being able to see it all was still very new to her, and she paused often to gaze about her at the mountains towering majestically towards the sky. Her glance swept over the lower peaks and down to the forest-like valleys below, and she drew the clean, sweet air deep into her lungs. She felt at that moment as if she did not have a care in the world, and the smile that started so tentatively in her eyes finally lifted the corners of her soft mouth. She had been fortunate, *very* fortunate, and, not for the first time, she thanked God for giving her the opportunity to see again.

'Good morning, green eyes,' a deep, familiar voice spoke directly behind her, and she turned to find herself looking up into James's mocking blue eyes. 'Did you dream of me?'

His taunting query added fuel to the fire of her sudden anger, and she clenched her hands at her sides as she glowered up at him. 'For heaven's sake, leave me alone!'

'Is that the way to talk to someone who wants only to help you?'

'A fat lot of help you will be,' she replied scathingly, swinging away from him with her head in the air, but the grass was wet with dew, and her feet slipped out from under her.

James made an attempt to save her from falling, but it was a disastrous effort. His feet slipped out from under him, just as hers had done, and they both went down with Roxy landing heavily on top of him. She was momentarily too stunned to do anything but stare down into his laughing eyes, then a strong hand cupped the back of her head, and her lips were brought down to meet his. There had been no time to think of resistance, and she found herself kissing him back with a matching warmth.

'This is a novel way of getting to know each other, I must say,' he laughed softly when he eventually allowed her a little breathing space.

'This is crazy,' she said, her voice unsteady with suppressed laughter as she tried to disengage herself from his arms, but they merely tightened about her.

'I agree with you. This is crazy,' he mocked her. 'Surely you could have thought of a more dignified way of flinging yourself into my arms?'

Her anger flared instantly, and she beat at his chest with her clenched fists. 'Oh, you *beast*! You——'

His hand reached up, bringing her head down to his, and his lips stifled the rest of her tirade as he rolled over with her in his arms until it was she who was lying beneath him among the wild grass and flowers.

His kiss lasted an eternity, stirring up a warmth within her that spread throughout her entire body to leave her limp and trembling as their bodies seemed to fuse together in one passionate flame. Coherent thought deserted her when his hands caressed her beneath her fleece-lined jacket, and her arms seemed to move of their own volition to become entwined about his neck in ecstatic surrender.

'You were saying?' he asked mockingly, nibbling at her ear when the storm inside them had subsided slightly.

A shiver of pleasure shot through her and she smiled dazedly. 'I can't remember. Can you?'

'Not a thing,' he assured her in an amused fashion before he subjected her to another intimate invasion of her mouth that sent a shudder of sensual desire through her. She felt vaguely uneasy about what was happening to her, but her uneasiness was swept aside by the emotions clamouring along her receptive bloodstream.

'Come on,' he said eventually, drawing her up with him and setting her firmly on her feet. 'Let's find ourselves a couple of horses and go for a long ride.'

'Oh, I couldn't,' she protested at once, still feeling a little lightheaded from his kisses. 'I haven't ridden a horse since——'

'Since?' he questioned abruptly when she paused and bit her lip nervously.

'Since I was a child of twelve.'

She recalled those carefree days with a feeling of nostalgia welling up within her. Her grandfather had owned several good riding horses and, on visits to his farm, she had often gone riding with her parents across the wild countryside in the shimmering heat of the day. It had given her a sense of freedom, and she had developed a deep love of nature that had dwindled only fractionally during those ten years of blindness.

She was aware suddenly of James eyeing her curiously, and she blushed guiltily when she realised that she had not heard a word he had said. 'I'm sorry,' she muttered apologetically. 'You were saying?'

'I asked if you were a good rider as a child.'

'Reasonably good, yes.'

'Then you'll soon get into the swing of it again,' he announced with a confidence she was far from experiencing.

Roxy was wearing slacks, so there was no need to change, and long before she had time to give in to her nervousness and doubts, she found herself seated astride a frisky brown mare with a gleaming coat. Memories came flooding back, and with it the knowledge she had thought forgotten. She began to move with the animal, instinct taking over, and soon she was riding at a comfortable gallop beside James on the black stallion he had selected for himself. The smell of horseflesh and creaking leather invaded her nostrils, and she felt peculiarly content, as if she had stepped back in time to enjoy the half-forgotten pleasures of her childhood.

'Enjoying it?' asked James, drawing his horse alongside hers when they slowed down to a trot.

She flashed him an uninhibited smile. 'I'd forgotten how wonderful it could be!'

The path narrowed ahead and led to a stream that wound its way amongst shady trees down into the valley, and James reined in his horse to allow her to go ahead of him.

'Let's rest the horses for a while,' he suggested when they had gone some distance further along the verge of the stream, and she reined in her horse willingly to rest for a moment in these peaceful surroundings.

She stretched out her legs and leaned back against the tree with her eyes closed. A little distance away the tethered horses nibbled at the grass, while the breeze rustled the leaves in the trees above her, and in these peaceful surroundings she could almost forget those disturbing shadows that lurked in her mind. She stirred at length to find James lying on his back beside her with an arm flung across his eyes, and she stared down at him contemplatively. His hair grew strongly back from his broad forehead, and she experienced the sudden desire to run her fingers through it, but she jerked her hand back moments later when he stirred and rolled over on to his side to meet her steady regard with his intensely blue eyes. She withstood his probing glance for a time, then she lowered her lashes and plucked nervously at a blade of grass which she twisted idly about her finger.

Her feelings for this man disturbed her, and there was a nagging familiarity about him which she had not been able to shake off from the moment he had held her in his arms on that day they had met high up on that rugged mountain when she had shared the magnificent view and his coffee with him.

'Have we ever met before?' she asked at last with a measure of pleading uncertainty in her voice.

'We may have,' he replied evenly, making no effort to pretend that he did not understand her as he propped himself up on one elbow. 'The possibility disturbs you, doesn't it?'

'I can't shake off the feeling that I've known you before.' She observed him closely, her eyes searching behind the tinted lenses, but his ruggedly handsome face remained expressionless. 'Am I completely wrong in thinking so?' she persisted urgently.

He was silent for a considerable length of time, and she began to think that he had no intention of replying to her query, but then, when she was about to repeat her question, he sighed and sat up with a casual arm resting on one raised knee.

'No, you're not wrong,' he said abruptly, and Roxy found it difficult to suppress the excitement that churned through her.

'We *have* met before, then?'

'Yes.'

'Often?'

'Quite often.'

She waited expectantly, her glance curious and searching, then she observed a little dryly, 'For one who has professed the desire to help me regain my memory, you're not forwarding much information, are you?'

His mouth twisted as if in a smile, but it never quite reached his eyes. 'I was warned to take care.'

'Warned?' she frowned, sitting up straight. 'Warned by whom?'

'Your father.'

'My father knew, then, who you were that first evening when we saw you at dinner here in the hotel?' she asked incredulously, watching his face intently, but it remained expressionless, and something cold began to twine itself about her heart.

'Your father knew, yes,' he admitted.

Her mouth twisted bitterly. 'I must say I never thought my father had it in him to be such an excellent actor!'

'Don't be annoyed with him,' James smiled faintly for the first time. 'We were both acting on Dr Gordon's and Dr Vaughn's advice.'

Suspicion became interwoven with bitterness as a picture of a different kind began to unfold before her. 'This little holiday was planned for me, then, between the four of you?'

'You could say so, yes,' James admitted readily, but when he saw the expression on her face he added quickly, 'We had only your own interests at heart, I assure you.'

'Then you have some kind of therapy in mind?' she probed with a new-found cynicism. 'Last night, for instance. Was that part of the planned therapy to help me regain those lost two months?'

He was on his knees beside her in an instant, his eyes burning angrily into hers, and his hands gripping her shoulders tightly. 'Dammit, Roxy, I could shake you!'

She waited for him to fit the action to the words, but instead he whipped off her glasses and dragged her up against him to kiss her with a thoroughness that left her breathless and dizzy.

'That wasn't done on anyone's instructions,' he blazed down at her when he raised his head. 'I've kissed you because I've had the desire to do so, and for no other reason. Given half a chance, I'd do much more than that.'

'Oh!' she gasped, colouring with acute embarrassment. 'We're back on the subject of seduction again.'

'By your own choice, yes, you little witch,' he laughed suddenly, and then she was being kissed in a way that drew a wild response from her.

Without taking his mouth from hers, he lowered her on to the grass and their bodies seemed to melt together. His hands were beneath her sweater, warm and persuasive against her skin, but she struggled beneath him when his fingers fumbled with the catch of her bra.

'Don't . . . please!' she begged, and he released her at once. She sat up and pushed unsteady fingers through her short auburn hair as she tried to reach beyond the shadows of her mind. 'Were we—I mean, was there——'

'We weren't lovers, if that's what you mean,' he laughed harshly. 'You were always a prickly customer at the best of times.'

Roxy digested this information with a feeling of relief while she observed him through lowered lashes. 'You know about my having an operation, of course.'

His mouth tightened. 'Yes, I know.'

'Why don't I remember you?' she asked, probing his strong features with a frowning concentration.

'You'll remember in time.'

'So everyone tells me, but I'm beginning to despair,' she sighed irritably, jumping to her feet and walking towards the edge of the stream where the overhanging branch of the tree almost touched the clear, swift-flowing water. 'It's been months now since I had that operation, and I still don't recall a thing about those weeks before I went into the clinic.'

'Don't worry about it, and don't try to force it,'

James advised, coming up behind her, and she swung round agitatedly to face him.

'Why didn't you tell me right from the start that we'd known each other?'

'Your father advised me not to.' His expression had become shuttered once more. 'He was afraid it might upset you, and I agreed to wait until a suitable opportunity arose to tell you.'

Roxy wondered suddenly how much was still being kept from her for fear of upsetting her, and she wondered, too, if James would know anything about the mysterious Marcus Fleming whom she was supposed to have known so well that her father had thought her in love with him. A coldness seemed to seep into her veins, and she shivered involuntarily. What kind of woman was she that she could have forgotten someone she was supposed to have loved? And what was this physical attraction she felt for a man she had known only a few days, but who now proclaimed that she had known him for some time before her operation? Had she perhaps been playing Marcus and James off against each other? Professing to love the one, while she found physical excitement with the other? Just how despicable had she become during those weeks she could not remember? The colour drained from her cheeks, and she swayed on her feet in the effort to remember, but the only result was that throbbing ache at her temples that made her wince inwardly.

Strong hands steadied her, and a deep voice said with unexpected gentleness, 'Take it easy, Roxy. It won't do any good to learn too much too soon. Be patient a little longer, and try to think of nothing other than making this a holiday to remember.'

Strangely enough, Roxy took his advice, and when James drove her back to Johannesburg in his Lamborghini at the end of those memorable two weeks, she felt relaxed and at ease, and no longer guilty at the way she reacted to the man seated beside her. She studied his strong profile with eyes that still carefully veiled her feelings, and she wondered once again how she could have forgotten a man with such a dynamic personality. She realised suddenly that, although he seemed to know so much about her, she knew virtually nothing about him. His authoritative manner indicated that he was a man in a position of leadership, but he could be a motor mechanic for all she knew.

Her glance travelled to the hands resting on the steering wheel. They were strong and competent hands with short, clean fingernails, and although they indicated that he had done some heavy work in his time, there was no indication that they were the hands of a labourer.

He turned his head briefly, and she blushed when she realised that she had been caught staring. His hand came down on to her knee, making her colour deepen when he asked casually, 'Are you comfortable?'

'How could one not be comfortable in a luxurious car such as this?'

His hand moved half way up her thigh with a deliberate sensuality before he returned it to the steering wheel and, as always, his touch had a shattering effect on her. Her pulses raced, her colour deepened, and it was some considerable time before she managed to control her rapid breathing.

They stopped for lunch along the way at a drive-in restaurant, and when they returned to the car to continue their journey, he helped her into her seat and leaned over her to fasten the seat belt. He did not move away at once, and kissed her long and lingeringly in full view of anyone who cared to notice, but she was too bemused to care at that moment what people might think.

Her heightened colour seemed to amuse him, and when he climbed in beside her and started the car, he smiled at her a little mockingly and said: 'I think what intrigues me most about you is the way you blush. Not many women do these days, but then most of them are married or have had affairs at your age, which does do away with some of those delightful virginal qualities men still hope to find in women.'

Roxy placed her cool hands against her hot cheeks as the Lamborghini picked up speed on the main road to Johannesburg. No man, as far as she could recall, had ever spoken to her as frankly as James had done about matters which she had never even dared to mention in front of her father, and never had her father uttered sexually inclined statements in her company. James, however, had spoken of rape, seduction, and virginity as if they were subjects one would normally discuss across the breakfast table, but there was more to it than that. His most innocent remarks, and everything about him, in fact, suggested to her a sensuality that excited her sexually in a way that alarmed her at times.

'Have I shocked you?' James interrupted her thoughts, and she lowered her hands swiftly to her lap.

'I've long since discovered that you seem to delight in shocking me,' she replied, averting her eyes.

'And I've discovered that you're as innocent as a babe where physical relationships between men and women are concerned,' he countered swiftly.

'Is that so terrible?'

'It's a rare occurrence these days, that's all,' he shrugged it off.

'I was brought up to believe in certain principles, and I suppose you would say I'm inhibited, but I can't change that—not even to be fashionable.'

'A pity.' His smile was brief and mocking. 'I would enjoy being your tutor if you should ever change your mind.'

Her throat tightened. 'What you're offering me is an affair, I take it?'

'Would you prefer a proposal of marriage?'

'No,' she replied at once, not quite sure why her heart should be beating so fast while she observed him closely. 'You're not the marrying sort. Besides, you like variety.'

Those last words echoed through her mind with a bruising familiarity, and she leaned back against her seat, pale and shaken as if she had seen a ghost. James glanced at her at that moment, and pulled the car off the road at once.

'What is it, Roxy?' he demanded, undoing his seat belt and leaning towards her with a hint of anxiety in his eyes.

'Someone said that once, but who, and where?' she whispered hoarsely, pressing her fingertips against her throbbing temples. 'Oh, if only I could remember!'

'Relax,' he ordered, taking her hands away from her face and placing an arm about her shoulders. 'Let it come naturally.'

She sat motionless for a moment, then she pressed her face into his broad, oddly comforting shoulder. 'James, I . . . I'm afraid.'

'Afraid of what?' he questioned, brushing his fingers lightly through her hair in a manner that soothed her considerably.

'I wish I knew, but . . .' She raised her head, then, and stared up into his face which was just centimetres from hers. 'Could it be that something happened—something so disturbing that I'm afraid to remember because it—it may have been painful?'

'It's possible,' he admitted grimly. 'Subconsciously, perhaps, you're afraid to face the truth, and it's your fear that may be preventing you from recalling that period before your operation.'

'Do you know of anything that may have happened?'

For a brief moment he looked uncomfortable, then he said abruptly, 'There was a misunderstanding.'

'Between you and me?' she asked, holding her breath.

'Yes.'

'Did we sort it out?'

'It has been sorted out, yes,' he said after another brief pause.

'And where does Marcus Fleming fit into those weeks I can't remember?' she asked, curious to know more, but James seemed to go white about the mouth before he released her and started the car.

'That you'll have to ask him,' he stated harshly, swinging the Lamborghini back on to the road and putting his foot down on the accelerator.

'Do you know Marcus Fleming?' she persisted doggedly, ignoring his obvious reluctance to discuss this shadowy figure from her past.

'Yes, I know him.'

'What's he like?'

'For God's sake, Roxy!' James exploded with a fury that made her pale visibly.

'I'm sorry,' she murmured apologetically, but, still not satisfied, she asked, 'Don't you like him, then?'

She saw the muscles in his jaw harden as if he were controlling his anger with difficulty. 'I don't like myself at the moment, so shut up and let me concentrate on my driving.'

Roxy did not question him further after that, and the rest of their journey was completed in a strained silence that made her suspect that James actually knew more than he was willing to tell her. It was all totally bewildering, and the more she thought about it, the more confused she became.

They arrived in Johannesburg late that afternoon, and when her rambling home with its whitewashed walls came into view, she could not suppress the shiver of excitement that rippled through her. Her father hurried down the steps to welcome them, but a golden labrador streaked past him and beat him to it.

'Sheba, you darling!' Roxy cried as she stepped out of the car and submitted to the tumultuous welcome from the faithful animal. Sheba whined and barked excitedly, wagging her tail at a furious pace, then she saw James taking Roxy's suitcase out of the trunk of the car, and, to Roxy's surprise, he received a similar welcome. Roxy hugged and kissed her father, then she turned once more to watch this phenomenon.

'That's odd,' she remarked at last. 'Sheba doesn't usually take to strangers with such enthusiasm, but then, I suppose, you're not a stranger to her.'

'No, I'm not, but she liked me from the start, and it was, perhaps, because she sensed that I happen to like animals,' James told her casually as he straightened and extended a hand towards her father. 'Good afternoon, Theodore.'

'Hello ... er ... James.' Her father cleared his throat selfconsciously as if something had embarrassed him. 'Thank you for taking care of Roxy and bringing her home safely.'

'It was my pleasure,' James smiled briefly.

'Hey!' Roxy exclaimed indignantly, glancing from one to the other and finally settling her green, accusing gaze on her father. 'You make that sound as though James had been employed to play nursemaid!'

'I wasn't employed to do anything of the kind,'

James intervened reprovingly. 'So stop being so prickly.'

'Come in and have something cool to drink,' Theodore interrupted hastily.

'Forgive me, but I must be on my way,' James declined the offer politely, then he glanced at Roxy, his expression unfathomable. 'I'll see you again.'

'James!' she cried anxiously, gripping his arm when he was about to turn towards his car. 'Do you mean that? You will come and see me again?'

'I'll see you again,' he repeated, smiling mockingly down into her eyes now as he carefully disengaged her hand from his arm. 'My therapy hasn't been successful yet, has it?'

Roxy watched the Lamborghini kicking up gravel as it sped down the drive, then her eyes clouded with pain. Was that the only reason he would want to see her again? Because he had not yet succeeded in helping her to regain her memory?

A hand touched her shoulder. 'Come inside, my dear. I'm longing to hear all about your holiday.'

She nodded absently, and Theodore picked up her suitcase in silence before escorting her into the house with Sheba following close at their heels.

CHAPTER TEN

TRUE to his word, and despite Roxy's misgivings, James spent a considerable amount of time with her during the three weeks following their return from the Drakensberg. He took her boating on the dam on two occasions, and they dined often at a restaurant in the city where the portly restaurateur, Carlo, welcomed her like an old friend. The veils shrouding her memory were being lifted one by one, and yet something vital remained missing; the link that joined it all together to make one whole. It was frustrating, but after a visit to Dr Gordon, she felt less anxious, and more confident about the immediate future.

It was while she was in Basil Vaughn's consulting-rooms for a check-up that she recalled something quite disturbing. He took her hands in his and raised them to his lips, using words that lifted the veil a little higher in her mind.

'You know how I feel about you,' he said, his pale grey eyes observing her intently when her expression registered shock, at first, and then dismay.

'Yes, I know,' she whispered, remembering every detail now of his proposal after they had attended a party at his golf club.

'Do you remember that I asked you once to marry me?' he asked quietly.

'I remember it now.'

His hands tightened about hers. 'Dare I hope that you might give me an answer soon?'

She lowered her eyes and shifted uncomfortably on the high stool which had brought her on a level with his height. She did not want to hurt him, but she knew she could not let him continue hoping for something she could not give him.

'I'm fond of you, Basil, but I could never marry you,' she finally broke the strained, expectant silence. 'I don't love you—not the way you would want me to—I'm sorry.'

He lowered his head over her hands and nodded slowly. 'I appreciate your honesty, but I've been a fool to keep on hoping when I've suspected all along that there's someone else.'

'Forgive me,' she whispered contritely.

'There's nothing to forgive,' he smiled selfconsciously. 'We're still friends, aren't we?'

'Oh, yes,' she said hastily, curling her fingers about his. 'You'll always be my very dear friend.'

He turned away then, and thrust his hands into the pockets of his white coat. 'How much have you remembered, Roxy?'

'Snatches here and there; little incidents that seem to have no relation to anything at all, as though I'm building a puzzle with every second piece missing.'

He picked up his pen and twisted it between his fingers while he studied her thoughtfully. 'Do you recall coming here and insisting that I do the operation?'

Another piece of the puzzle jolted into place, and she nodded. 'I remember that now, but I can't think why I should have been so insistent.'

'You said that you'd reached the end, and that it didn't matter to you one way or the other.'

'Did I give you any idea why I should have felt that way?' she asked after a startled pause.

'You refused to give an explanation when I asked for one.'

Roxy felt more than ordinarily disturbed, but she knew from past experience that it would do no good to brood, or to endeavour to probe deeper into the shadows that still lurked in her mind, so she shrugged it off with a sigh.

'I suppose I shall remember it all in time,' she echoed the advice everyone was always passing on to her and, picking up her handbag, she prepared to leave his rooms. 'When do I have to see you again?'

'In a month's time for the final check-up,' he said,

glancing at his desk calendar before he looked up and added with professional severity, 'It's important, so make a note of it.'

Roxy drove herself home that morning in the Peugeot with Maggie keeping a watchful eye beside her. She had improved rapidly since her first driving lesson under Maggie's expert supervision, and soon, she hoped, she would obtain her driver's licence. It gave her a wonderful sense of freedom to be able to drive herself where she wanted to be, and it did wonders for her bruised independence.

She sat out on the terrace after lunch that day to soak up the sun, but her peace was disturbed when Sheba growled beside her. Roxy placed a restraining hand on her collar, and looked up to see a pretty, dark-haired girl coming up the steps towards her, but she failed to identify her visitor until the girl spoke.

'Well, well, well,' she said with characteristic petulance tinged with sarcasm. 'So I get to see you at last.'

'Hello, Vera,' Roxy smiled, gesturing towards the chair opposite her own while she took in the appearance of her elegantly clad visitor and tried to decide whether she was disappointed or not. 'What do you mean—*at last*?'

'Well, your father and Maggie have been guarding you as if you were a precious piece of china,' Vera explained with that familiar touch of sarcasm as she seated herself, and Roxy heard the faint swish of her nylons as she carefully crossed her shapely legs. 'Absolutely no visitors, they said.'

'I didn't know,' Roxy murmured with dawning comprehension.

Vera's dark eyes slid down to the golden labrador sitting up in a watchful attitude beside Roxy's chair. 'Your dog has never liked me either.'

'Sheba means no harm,' Roxy assured her defensively, her hand caressing the animal's head. 'She's merely protective.'

Vera studied Roxy thoughtfully, then she asked in her usual candid manner, 'Can you actually see me?'

'I can see you very clearly,' Roxy replied, inwardly amused.

Vera shivered. 'It makes me feel a bit peculiar knowing that.'

'Why should it?' Roxy asked, a little startled, sliding her glance over the perfectly proportioned figure in the narrow green skirt and matching jacket, but it was the full, rather petulant mouth that told her most of what she had wanted to know. 'You're almost exactly as I imagined you would be.'

Vera stared at her a little suspiciously, but Roxy's calm expression gave no indication of her thoughts at that moment.

'What have you been doing with yourself since your operation?' Vera asked eventually.

'Nothing much,' Roxy shrugged. 'I went away for two weeks, but since my return I've been learning to drive a car, and I'm thinking of studying part-time for my law degree.'

'Aren't you a bit too old for that?'

'I don't think so,' Roxy argued. 'I was twenty-three two months ago, but one is never too old to further one's education.'

'I've been away myself. Only returned a few days ago from a month's holiday in Switzerland,' Vera explained, fingering the wide pleat in her skirt, then she raised her slightly narrowed glance to Roxy's. 'I saw Marcus last night.'

'Marcus?' Roxy questioned uneasily, trying to understand why Vera's mention of that name should disturb her so much.

'I forgot. You've lost your memory, I'm told,' Vera smiled a little sarcastically. 'Just as well, perhaps. He was dining with a divine-looking blonde, and they appeared to be terribly chummy.'

'It makes no difference to me who—who this man dines with,' Roxy explained haltingly. 'I don't recall him at all.'

'As I said—just as well,' Vera smiled again that twisted, spiteful little smile, then she added with what could only be described as satisfaction, 'There are rumours of marriage doing the rounds of the social circles. No one seems to know who the lucky girl is going to be, but my bet is that it's the blonde I saw him with last night.'

Roxy experienced an unexpected stab of pain for which she could find no explanation, and she was speechless with concentration while she tried desperately to remember.

'Telephone for you, Miss Roxy,' Maggie interrupted from the french windows leading out on to the terrace, but Vera rose elegantly to her feet before Roxy could motivate herself into action.

'Oh, well, you must excuse me,' she smiled, adding a little confidentially, 'I have a super date for this evening, and I'm on my way to the hairdresser's.'

Roxy stared after her for a moment before going inside to take the call. She wondered excitedly whether it would be James, but when she lifted the receiver it was her father's voice explaining that he would not be in to dinner that evening, and that she was not to wait up for him. She assured him that she would be perfectly all right, but she spent a disturbing afternoon brooding over the conversation she had had with Vera Sinclair. The call she had expected from James did not materialise either, and the thought of spending the evening alone did not appeal to her.

She wanted to telephone James to invite him to spend the evening with her, but she had never thought to ask for his number, and he had never proffered it. It seemed a little strange, now that she thought of it, but she went through to her father's study after dinner that evening, and undauntedly searched through the directory for the number she required. She knew that James had a flat in the city, but there was only one J. Allen listed in the book, and he lived somewhere in Parktown.

'Damn!' she muttered to herself, fingering the directory idly, then, on an inexplicable impulse, she paged on towards the F's and slid her finger casually down the columns until she encountered the surname 'Fleming'. There were several, but one in particular jarred her mind violently. The initials were 'M.J.A.' and the flat number was '603'.

Something inside her clamoured for release, and the perspiration stood out on her forehead when she picked up the receiver and dialled the number that was indicated. She had to know. *She had to!*

For several frightening seconds she heard nothing except the persistent ringing of the telephone at the other end, and the thundering beat of her own heart, then a feminine voice answered and asked who was calling.

It was a well-modulated and faintly musical voice that struck deep into Roxy's brain with an agonising precision that made the room spin wildly about her, then, as if to clarify the memories that came rushing back into her mind with the force of a hurricane, the receiver was taken from the woman and a man's voice demanded sharply, 'Who is that?'

Roxy replaced the receiver swiftly with hands that shook when she felt the blood drain from her face, then the carpeted floor of her father's study threatened to rise up and meet her, but she clutched at the desk and leaned against it heavily with her head bowed until the tumultuous soaring ceased in her ears.

The shutters in her mind had opened like floodgates, and the missing pieces of the puzzle now tumbled into place, each one of them stabbing at her soul with renewed and agonising vigour. She had been duped once again by a man who cared no more for her than he cared for all the other women who came and went in his life, but the most hurtful part of it all was the fact that her father, the one person she had trusted above all others, had played a significant role in this final, most humiliating deception.

God, they had been clever, she thought bitterly as she left the study and went up to her room. 'But not clever enough,' a little voice told her. 'The final scene is yours to play as you wish.'

There was little comfort in that thought, but during the long sleepless hours of the night she began to realise its potential. She would play their game a little while longer, then, at the appropriate moment, she would have her revenge, and she promised herself that it would be sweet.

James telephoned her early the following morning and invited her to have dinner with him that evening, and she naturally accepted at once. There was something of importance he wished to discuss with her, he had said, and she could well imagine that he was beginning to feel the pinch of the dual roles he was playing.

Roxy dressed with care that evening, and selected her new emerald green evening gown of soft, embroidered silk. The neckline plunged a little daringly, but it enhanced the beauty of her slender neck and smooth, creamy shoulders. Her auburn hair had grown considerably over the past weeks, and in the light above the dressing-table it shone with a touch of gold as she brushed it into that new sweeping style which had been recommended by her hairdresser. The eyes that met hers in the mirror looked calm and steady, almost as if they belonged to someone else, and they hid successfully the nervousness and tension which seemed to have taken possession of every muscle and every nerve in her body.

The evening did not progress quite as she had imagined it would. She found herself staring with mixed feelings at the man seated opposite her, and endlessly had to remind herself of his treachery when her hungry yearning for him overruled her bitterness and deep-seated anger. The forcefulness of his strong personality was etched deeply in her heart and mind, and she wondered now how she could have forgotten his existence so completely over the past months.

Piercing blue eyes probed her shuttered glance, and a frown appeared between the heavy brows. 'Is something troubling you, Roxy?'

'Why should there be something troubling me?' she demanded with forced casualness.

'You've been very quiet this evening—almost preoccupied.' His hand found hers across the table, and that familiar current of awareness passed through her as he leaned towards her anxiously. 'You're not feeling ill, are you?'

'No,' she shook her head, trying to decide whether his concern was genuine, or part of the act. 'I've never felt better,' she added with a hint of flippancy in her voice.

He released her hand and leaned back in his chair to observe her with a brooding expression on his face. His rapier-sharp eyes travelled from her new hairstyle down to the seductive hollow between her breasts before it swept upwards to her face once more as if searching for something.

'You're different, somehow,' he admitted at last, and she smiled inwardly with cynical satisfaction.

'I feel different,' she admitted with care.

His glance sharpened perceptibly. 'Something happened to make you feel this way?'

'One could say so, yes,' she said, bitterness curving her usually soft mouth.

'Want to tell me about it?' he asked, his eyes watchful.

'Later, perhaps,' she waved aside the subject. 'I believe there was something you wanted to discuss with me?'

'That can wait as well,' he said with an odd, almost haunted expression in his eyes. 'More coffee?'

'No, thank you.'

His mouth tightened ominously. 'Shall we go, then?'

'I think so.'

He ushered her out of the continental atmosphere of Carlo's restaurant and into the cool March night to where he had parked his dark-green Lamborghini, and she welcomed its plush interior when her legs began to shake beneath her. The engine purred to life, and the car slid into the traffic under the expert guidance of those strong hands at the wheel. Roxy knew what she had to do, it had all been rigidly planned beforehand, but in the intimately confined space of his car she felt her senses sharpening at his nearness. Her mind remained hard and unforgiving, but her treacherous heart throbbed with a warmth and longing to know the touch of his lips. She wanted to feel those muscled arms about her just once more before she walked out of his life for the last time.

The car turned off to the left after the traffic lights had stopped them, and her mind cleared with a sharp jolt. 'This isn't the way to my home,' she said accusingly.

'I'm not taking you home.'

He had spoken calmly yet decisively, but there had been something in his voice that had sent a trickle of fear coursing up her spine, and she glanced at him warily, taking in the rigid contours of his face in the dashboard light.

'May I know where you're taking me?' she asked at last, passing the tip of her tongue nervously over her dry lips.

'I'm taking you to my flat.' The words grated jarringly along her nerves, and left her momentarily speechless. He turned his head to glance at her briefly, then he asked mockingly, 'No comment?'

'I'm surprised you've waited this long before taking me there,' she replied with a bravado she was far from experiencing.

'Had I known you wouldn't object I would have done so some time ago,' he continued to mock her, but when no flippant reply came to her rescue, he asked, 'Does the thought of being alone with me in my flat frighten you, or excite you?'

She looked at him then, and said with appropriate casualness, 'I haven't made up my mind about that yet.'

'You're a cool customer this evening, I must say,' he laughed, but the sound was harsh and frightening, and she lapsed into a silence which lasted until he drove his car down into the basement of a building that was new to her, and yet familiar.

The lift took them at a sickening pace from the basement up to the sixth floor, but anything was preferable to being closeted in that small steel cage with this man whom she loved yet feared. He had hurt her more than she had imagined possible, and he would hurt her again without the slightest compunction if she did not guard against it.

Hard fingers latched on to her arm as the doors slid open. If thoughts of escape had perhaps occurred to her, then he gave her no opportunity to do so, and she was steered swiftly towards the panelled door on their right. Ten paces, Maggie had told her that fateful night which now seemed to have drifted an eternity into the past, but in her ridiculously high-heeled sandals it took her several paces more before they reached the door. His key turned silently in the lock, and seconds later she found herself in the modern interior of what appeared to be a solely masculine domain. It was furnished in leather and solid wood, the colours ranging from a deep tobacco brown to a pale creamy beige, and nowhere was there the slightest evidence that a woman had shared the flat with him the night before. She could not say the same for the bedrooms, naturally, but in the lounge itself not a sign of a feminine presence was visible.

Roxy was gestured into a wide, padded armchair while he crossed the room towards the oak cupboard against the wall. He took out two glasses, and from the small, built-in refrigerator he produced a bottle of champagne. She watched in surprised fascination while he undid the wrapper and eased off the cork, but she averted her glance when he looked up at her unexpectedly with a sardonic gleam in his eyes. The cork shot off loudly, jolting her nerves, and then he was pouring the sparkling liquid into the glasses.

'What are we celebrating?' she asked suspiciously when a glass was placed in her trembling hand.

'Who knows?' he shrugged, his mocking eyes raking over her slender, taut frame. 'Before this night is over we may find we have something to celebrate.'

Her cheeks flamed, and her hand shook to such an extent that she was forced to hold the glass with both hands for fear of spilling the liquid into her lap. 'Did you bring me here to seduce me?'

'That's usually why I bring women here,' he smiled cynically, placing his glass on the low table between them and turning towards the hi-fi which was built into the shelves against the wall. 'Shall I put on a record? Something, perhaps, that will smooth your ruffled feathers and make it easier for me?'

'What about Beethoven's Appassionata?' she suggested stiffly, recalling with agonising poignancy the music she had heard coming from his flat that night when she had paid him such an untimely and unwanted visit.

'Good choice,' he remarked, placing the record on the turntable, and moments later the familiar, nostalgic music filled the room.

'What shall we drink to?' she asked nervously when he picked up his glass and stood staring down at her with a speculative gleam in those intensely blue eyes.

'To us,' he said at once, but she stopped him before the glass reached his lips.

'I would rather drink to something more specific.'

'Such as?' he smiled down at her.

This was the moment she had waited for, but now that the stage was set, she was afraid, and she had to grab hold of her faltering courage before it deserted her entirely. She rose to her feet and, with a cynical smile playing about her mouth, lifted her glass in salute.

'Let's drink to the end of a superbly played masquerade, Marcus James Allen Fleming,' she stated in cold, precise tones, and she had the satisfaction of seeing his ruggedly tanned features darken to a dull red before the blood drained away to leave him peculiarly pale.

He flicked a switch and the music ceased abruptly, then his voice exploded hoarsely into the electrifying silence. 'You know?'

'Yes, I'm afraid I do.'

'Everything?'

'Yes.'

His eyes, dark and fathomless in his white face, probed hers. 'When did this happen?'

'Last night,' she said abruptly, her throat working with the effort to control the bitter tears which rose and threatened to choke her. 'Why didn't you tell me who you really were?'

His glass, untouched, followed hers down on to the low table between them. 'Believe it or not, I was afraid to,' he said at last, the muscles jerking in his jaw. 'After the way you reacted in the clinic I was afraid that knowing my true identity might upset you further.'

'So you became James Allen,' she laughed unsteadily, but in her heart there was no laughter, only pain and bitter disillusionment. 'It was very clever of you, I must say, and what fun you must have had laughing at my ignorance!'

'Roxy . . .'

'Tell me one thing,' she interrupted him swiftly. 'How did you explain me away to your lady friend?'

His eyes narrowed. 'What lady friend are you referring to?'

'Oh, yes,' she laughed cynically, turning away from him so that he would not see the agony mirrored in her eyes. 'I'd forgotten there could possibly be several women in your life, but the one I'm referring to is the one who was here that evening when I came to see you with the misguided hope of explaining away the misunderstanding which had occurred between us. She was here again last night, and I presume that it's the same woman you dined with two evenings ago.'

'You presume correctly,' he told her coldly. 'How did you discover this?'

'Vera Sinclair happened to see you dining together the other evening, and . . .' she swallowed convulsively. 'It was I who telephoned last night.'

'I see,' he remarked in that same, coldly detached voice. 'Why did you ring this number?'

'I was alone at home, and I looked up this number when I couldn't find your name in the telephone directory,' she replied with a bitter honesty that seemed to be wrenched from her very soul. 'Two things struck me simultaneously—the flat number and your initials. I became more than just suspicious, and I dialled the number out of curiosity. When I heard that—that woman's voice, I knew, and when you took the receiver from her to speak into it, my mind cracked wide open to—to the deception you and my father have practised with such care. I knew everything; every hateful detail of every deceitful incident, and I—I think I despise you both for humiliating me in this way.'

'It was never our intention to humiliate you.'

'Oh, no, of course not,' she exclaimed, swinging round to face him and flashing him a glance filled with angry sarcasm. 'You were both merely concerned with assisting the restoration of my memory, and while I'm certain that my father had only that in mind, *you* had to take it a bit further. You wanted to derive as much personal pleasure out of the situation, and you did so without regard for my feelings once the truth were known.'

'Roxy, listen to me.'

'No, *you* listen to *me*!' she cried with the bitter taste of gall in her mouth as she brushed off his hands, and stared up at him with eyes filling with the stinging moisture of angry tears. 'I've taken about as much as I can stand from the people I believed I could trust, but

I hate and despise you most of all for your deceit, and I hope I never have to see you again!'

She picked up her purse and fled towards the door, intent upon leaving before she burst into tears and made a complete fool of herself, but hard, punishing hands gripped her shoulders in a vice and she was thrust violently into a chair.

'*Sit down!*' he snarled at her, thrusting her back into the chair when she tried to brush off his hands in order to escape.

'How dare you treat me like this!' she demanded.

'I'll treat you any damn way I please, Roxana Cunningham,' he told her harshly, his lips drawn back against his teeth in an angry snarl, and she shrank from the fury in his eyes when he leaned over her threateningly with his hands on the arms of her chair. 'If you think you're the only one who's been living under the pressure of strain these past months, then you're mistaken. At first I had to put up with your touchiness because of your blindness, and the barricade you'd erected because of your ridiculous idea that you could never be more than a burden to a man. Then there was that stupid misunderstanding that plunged me into the depths of hell. I went a little mad, I think, and for a time I considered settling in South America, but when I finally discovered the truth I found I was too late to prevent you from taking a step which could have killed you as certainly as it had cured you. *God*, Roxy,' he groaned white-faced, moving away from her and pushing his hands through his crisp hair, 'I don't think you'll ever know what I felt like when I rushed into that clinic to discover that the operation had been in progress since thirty minutes before my arrival. I aged years while I sat there in that infernal waiting-room with your father, and then, when you were told I wanted to see you, you collapsed hysterically and wiped me out of your memory along with a lot of other things.'

She stared up at him in complete bewilderment. She had never before seen him look so disturbed, so utterly distraught and tormented, but there was still too much bitterness churning through her.

'You surely didn't expect a welcome from me after that humiliating experience I'd suffered at your hands?' she demanded coldly. 'I swallowed my pride and came to see you—to explain—but you sent me away. You had a woman with you, and I was no one of importance.'

'Do you think I haven't suffered because of the way I treated you in my anger that night?' he stormed at her with a harshness that made her flinch inwardly. 'For months I had to sit back nursing my guilt while I was allowed only to watch you from a distance, and you'll never know what I've gone through these past weeks as James Allen. Roxy, I could shake you!' he thundered at her, his eyes blazing down into hers as he gripped her by the shoulders and lifted her almost bodily out of the chair so that she landed heavily against the hard wall of his chest. 'Don't you know that I love you, that I love every hair on your beautiful head, every bone in your delectable body, every inflection in your voice, your eyes, your touch. Oh, God, I'm like a man who's lost all sense of direction unless you're there to give purpose to my life, Roxy.'

He was saying incredibly wonderful things, but could she believe him? Dared she? she wondered as she avoided his descending lips. 'What about that woman who was here with you last night?' she demanded suspiciously. 'Where does she fit into your plans if you can say these things to me and expect me to believe you?'

A smile curved his stern mouth as his hands slid from her shoulders down to her waist. 'The woman who answered the telephone last night is Gail Rivers, and she's my sister.'

'Your sister!' she gasped incredulously.

'Her husband, Nigel, farms up north, and Gail makes a habit of invading my flat when she comes down to Johannesburg on her shopping sprees.'

'Oh, Marcus!' she groaned, leaning against him to hide the tears of relief that filled her eyes.

'Contrary to what you may have thought, this has been a strictly male domain since the day we met. There have been only two exceptions—my sister, and now yourself.'

'What can I say?' she whispered contritely, cursing herself for having had so little faith in him, and for the unnecessary unhappiness she had caused both Marcus and herself.

'You could try telling me that I haven't hoped in vain that you might one day learn to care for me,' he suggested wryly, lifting her face to his and brushing away her tears with his lips.

'But you know I love you,' she cried without hesitation, raising her tear-stained eyes to his and allowing him for the first time to see what lay in their depths. 'I've loved you desperately for so long. That's why it all hurt so much to think that you were merely amusing yourself with me.'

'I ought to punish you for that,' he ground out the words, and then she was being kissed as she had never been kissed before. There was tenderness and passion, and finally a driving need that drove them deeper into each other's arms until she returned his kisses with a matching hunger. 'Darling,' he groaned at last, drawing his lips from hers to bury them against her throat where her pulse leapt wildly. 'Tell me again that you love me.'

'I love you—very much. So much,' she added unsteadily, 'that I'll do whatever you ask of me, and I'll be whatever you want me to be.'

For a moment he did not react, then he drew away from her slightly to stare down at her quizzically. 'Are you offering me your sweet body, Roxy?'

A hot wave of colour surged into her cheeks, but she held his mocking glance unwaveringly. 'If that's what you want of me, yes.'

During the ensuing silence she recalled that he had once stated that he preferred variety to marriage, and if marriage was excluded from what he had to offer her, then she loved him enough to accept it.

'The temptation is irresistible, but I want much more than that,' he said at last, a warmth and tenderness in his eyes she had never seen there before, and a peculiar weakness invaded her limbs. 'I want more than the occasional stolen hour or two in bed with you,' he was saying, his voice vibrating with emotion. 'I want you there at night when I go to sleep, and when I awake in the morning, but most of all I want you there as my wife.'

'Marcus ...' Her voice broke with the incredible happiness flooding through her. Unashamedly she tightened her arms about his neck and showered him with kisses while she whispered brokenly, 'Oh, Marcus, I can't think of anything I want more than to be your wife.'

'It will have to be soon, though,' he warned sternly when he eventually released her from another soul-searching kiss which had created delicious havoc with her emotions. 'I don't enjoy living the life of a celibate, and I've been doing so since that day you walked all over me on the way to your father's office.'

She stared at him in disbelief. 'Dare I believe you?'

'You'd better,' he warned, his eyes darkening with

desire as he drew her down on to the sofa. 'How soon will you marry me?'

His fingers trailed a path of destruction from her throat down to the shadowy hollow between her breasts, and her voice quivered with suppressed emotion when she said: 'I'll marry you as soon as you wish.'

'What about this evening?' he suggested surprisingly, his fingers exploring boldly now beneath the embroidered silk bodice, and her body responded wildly to his touch.

'That's crazy,' she protested even though she agreed silently with every fibre of her being.

'Perhaps it is crazy,' he admitted, his sensuous mouth moving with delicious insistence across her smooth shoulder where his impatient hand had already brushed aside the narrow strap of her dress. 'The necessary documents have been lying in my desk drawer for days now, and there's a magistrate living two floors up, so why should we wait?'

'I hate to think what my father will say if I agree to this,' she whispered tremulously, and more than half way to agreeing.

'Telephone him and invite him over, but don't be surprised when you discover that he's given his consent to our marriage weeks ago.'

'Are you serious?' she demanded incredulously, struggling free of his lips and hands in order to think clearly.

'Absolutely serious,' Marcus nodded, stretching out a hand towards the telephone and extending the receiver towards her. 'Want to give him a call?'

Devilment lurked in her eyes as she shook her head and said: 'Make the necessary arrangements first. Your magistrate may be unwilling to perform a wedding ceremony at this late hour.'

He smiled triumphantly and kissed her hard on the mouth. 'I'll double his fee.' A few minutes later he replaced the receiver and turned to her with a look of satisfaction on his face. 'It's all arranged for eleven-thirty.'

Was she mad agreeing to marry him in such a frantic hurry? she wondered breathlessly, losing herself in the blue depths of his eyes, but the thought of having to go through the usual engagement period before the eventual marriage was too much even for her to bear.

Marcus leaned towards her urgently and, almost as if he had read her thoughts, he said: 'Why waste unnecessary time? We've known each other long enough, and we both know we'll never make it through a three-week engagement.'

She coloured and nodded silently, her eyes luminous and unshadowed for the first time in many months as she got up and stepped over his long legs to reach the telephone. She hesitated only briefly before lifting the receiver and dialling her father's number at home, and it rang for a considerable time before he answered it.

'Daddy, I thought I should let you know I'm spending the night with Marcus at his flat,' she stated mischievously, laughing silently down into Marcus's eyes when her father spluttered and exploded over the telephone, then, when the opportunity arose, she added calmly, 'If you want to be in time to witness our marriage, then you'd better get yourself here in a hurry. You have an hour.'

She returned the receiver to its cradle and thought a little wickedly, 'Let him stew a while in that!' but she giggled uncontrollably when she glanced at Marcus to find him shaking with silent laughter. She was pulled down into his arms the next instant to be kissed with an intensity that left her flushed and trembling.

'I think you've forgotten something,' she said at last and, when he raised a quizzical eyebrow, she added: 'A wedding ring.'

'Want to bet?' he demanded with that familiar mocking smile as he set her aside. He left the room and returned a few seconds later with a circle of gold between his forefinger and thumb which he held up for her inspection. 'One wedding ring as requested.'

'You've thought of everything, it seems,' she remarked a little dryly. 'I'm beginning to suspect that this evening is developing exactly as you planned it.'

Marcus sobered at once and pocketed the ring before he joined her on the sofa. 'On Gail's advice I planned to inform you of my true identity this evening. What happened after that I was prepared to leave entirely up to you.'

Several thoughts raced through her mind at once, but only one seemed to deserve her immediate attention, and she glanced up at him frowningly. 'Who told you about the note I'd received which cancelled our appointment?'

'Carlo,' he told her grimly. 'I questioned Maggie afterwards, and between us we came to the conclusion that Vera Sinclair was the only one who could possibly have sent that note. It didn't take much to get Vera to admit it either.'

'Like everyone else, Vera practised her own deceit,' Roxy sighed with a touch of sadness.

'She's spiteful and spoiled,' Marcus confirmed, placing a finger beneath her chin and raising her face to his. 'You're not still hating us for deceiving you a little, are you?'

'It would serve you right if I changed my mind this minute about marrying you, don't you think?' she teased.

'You little wretch,' he grunted, his arms threatening to crush her ribs to a pulp while his mouth found hers with a sensuality that drove coherent thought from her mind as he manoeuvred her into a reclining position on the sofa.

Her zip offered no resistance when his fingers tugged at it, and it slid down smoothly to bare her back. The expertise of those caressing hands against her skin made her tremble responsively, and soon the fire of her desire was kindled. She clung to him weakly, her total surrender urging him on until she was conscious only of drifting on a cloud of sweet, throbbing ecstasy.

The chime of a bell penetrated her dulled senses and she stirred uneasily beneath him, but it was only when the chime was repeated that his hands stilled against the rounded fullness of her breasts. Desire still smouldered in his eyes when he drew away from her, and he smiled that faintly mocking smile that no longer had the power to hurt her as he zipped her into her dress.

'Saved by the bell,' he said thickly, getting to his feet and striding towards the door.

'Would somebody mind telling me what's going on?' Theodore demanded a few moments later, pinning his daughter down with a severe glance when she rose unsteadily to her feet. 'Roxy?'

Outwardly calm, but inwardly floundering in the wake of her aroused emotions, her explanation came tumbling out, and there was a dash of mockery thrown in for good measure. 'I've remembered everything, and Marcus and I have discussed the matter, and we've decided not to waste unnecessary time in legalising our affair, which I trust will last until the end of our lives.'

She coloured and felt a little foolish during the ensuing silence until Marcus placed his arm about her

shoulders and remarked dryly, 'Only a woman, Theodore, has that uncanny ability to string half a dozen
statements into one sentence without so much as paus-
ing for breath.'

'And only a woman would expect to be understood,'
Theodore nodded exasperatedly.

'Only a woman as happy as I am at this moment
would refrain from doing you both a physical injury,'
Roxy intervened sharply, regaining her composure.

'Roxy, my dear,' her father smiled, holding out his
arms, and when she stepped into them he held her
tightly and kisssd her with sincere warmth. 'This is
not at all the kind of wedding I'd visualised for you,
but I'm happy with whatever you have decided.'

The magistrate arrived a few minutes later. He was a
short, stout little man with inquisitive eyes and an irritating twitch in his left shoulder, but they were
married fifteen minutes later, and the necessary docu-
ment to prove it was safely tucked away in Marcus's
wallet.

A fresh bottle of champagne was opened, and an hour
later Roxy found herself alone with Marcus, with
empty champagne glasses littering the small tables in
the living-room, and a gold band fitting snugly on her
finger to indicate her new status. This must be a
dream, she told herself. How could an evening that had
started out so badly end in such a joyously happy way?

She withstood the intense scrutiny of her newly
acquired husband's eyes, and laughed a little unsteadily when she felt her cheeks grow warm. 'This
has really been the most unconventional wedding, but
I don't think I would have had it any other way.'

His eyes glinted humorously. 'Ours has been an
unconventional courtship, and it's too late now to do
anything about it.'

'Do you realise that, in the rush, neither of us gave a thought to the fact that I'm here without a change of clothing?' She gestured towards the evening gown she was wearing, and raised her eyebrows in an expression of mock horror. 'Can you imagine the conclusion people will jump to in the morning when they see me walk out of here in this?'

'Who cares?' he demanded, his deep voice vibrating with an undercurrent of sensuality that made her pulse quicken receptively as he took her hands in his and drew her against him until his lips brushed against her forehead. 'I could always lend you a toothbrush, and for tonight, my sweet wife, you won't need clothes.'

Her faint gasp of embarrassment died beneath his lips and, lifting her in his arms, Marcus carried her through to his bedroom where, with infinite gentleness and care, he removed her clothes and proceeded to transform her into a fulfilled, drowsily content woman.

Everything had happened too swiftly for her to develop pre-wedding nerves, but she was glad of that now as she snuggled closer to his hard, muscular body and slid her hand across his hair-roughened chest.

'I love you very much, Marcus James Allen Fleming,' she murmured against his throat, and his arms tightened about her instantly.

'And I love you, Roxana Fleming, and don't ever doubt that,' he replied throatily, seeking her mouth with his.

They talked for a long time in hushed whispers, dispersing the doubts which had cast a shadow on their earlier relationship before her operation, then he made love to her once more, and she was awakened to the sensual delights she had never known existed until he had taken command of her untutored body. Now, a little wiser than before, she responded with an eager warmth, and his expertise as a lover took her to the peak of desire and beyond until she was delivered once again into that world of cascading sensations that made her cling to him helplessly in the aftermath of passion.

'God, Roxy,' he groaned, the burning warmth of his lips travelling from her throat to her breast. 'If I lived a thousand years it wouldn't be long enough to tell you how much I love you.'

What need was there of words when actions spoke so much clearer? she thought, tenderness flowing from her stroking fingertips as they found joy in exploring his broad shoulders and muscled back. He was hers and no one else's, and it was with this thought that those weeks and months of agonising misery faded into oblivion when she finally drifted sleepily in his strong, protective arms.

Harlequin Plus

A WORD ABOUT THE AUTHOR

Yvonne Whittal grew up in South Africa, spending her summers on the coast and her winter months inland at a sheep farm in the Karoo region. It was there that Yvonne came to know the farmers who loved the earth and faced a never ending struggle for survival. Her first novel, *East to Barryvale* (Romance #1915, published in 1975), was inspired by the people of the area.

Yvonne began scribbling stories at a very early age, and in her teens she considered writing as a profession. But marriage and three daughters caused her to shelve that idea...for a while.

Then, rusty after so many years away from her writing, Yvonne enrolled in a fiction-writing course and set to work. She began with short stories and moved on to a novel, which took several months to complete. "Fortunately," she laughingly comments on her slow start, "I did not have to make a living out of my writing then. Otherwise, I would surely have starved!"

Now's your chance to discover the earlier
books in this exciting series.

Choose from this list of great
SUPERROMANCES!

SUPERROMANCE

Complete and mail this coupon today!

- -

Harlequin Reader Service

In the U.S.A.
1440 South Priest Drive
Tempe, AZ 85281

In Canada
649 Ontario Street
Stratford, Ontario N5A 6W2

Please send me the following SUPERROMANCES. I am enclosing my check or money order for $2.50 for each copy ordered, plus 75¢ to cover postage and handling.

- ☐ #1 END OF INNOCENCE
- ☐ #2 LOVE'S EMERALD FLAME
- ☐ #3 THE MUSIC OF PASSION
- ☐ #4 LOVE BEYOND DESIRE
- ☐ #5 CLOUD OVER PARADISE
- ☐ #6 SWEET SEDUCTION
- ☐ #7 THE HEART REMEMBERS
- ☐ #8 BELOVED INTRUDER

Number of copies checked @ $2.50 each = $_____
N.Y. and Ariz. residents add appropriate sales tax $_____
Postage and handling $_____.75

                TOTAL $_____

I enclose_____.
(Please send check or money order. We cannot be responsible for cash sent through the mail.)
Prices subject to change without notice.

NAME_____
                     (Please Print)

ADDRESS_____

CITY_____

STATE/PROV._____

ZIP/POSTAL CODE_____

Offer expires May 31, 1982

109563323